fine
wine

Emem Bassey

First Published in Great Britain in 2020 by
LOVE AFRICA PRESS
103 Reaver House, 12 East Street, Epsom KT17 1HX
www.loveafricapress.com

ISBN: 9781916362840
Also available as paperback

ACKNOWLEDGEMENT

God is always first!

To Kiru Taye and Love Africa Press, thank you for believing in this series. You have no idea how happy I am to belong to the LAP family. It means a lot to me and I look forward to more great stories between us.

To my editor, Kaitesi, much hugs and kisses for making the process fun.

To that random, sexy older man model who's pictures made my head spin, thank you for the inspiration to create this series.

To Peter Bassey, for your support always. I would never exchange you for another.

To my mom and siblings and niece - I love you!

To Book reviews by Modus, your sexy, silver fox is here. Thank you for your anticipation, it meant I wasn't crazy to write this story.

To everyone who has contributed to the success of this book, pre and post production, thank you, so much!

DEDICATION

To all the assured women who know what and who they want despite societal pressures.

And to the other women who wish to be assured, may courage fill your lovely hearts.

CHAPTER ONE

"So, you're saying younger men are useless?"

Sifon groaned with a smile, rolling her eyes at her best friend. "That isn't what I meant. Older men are referred to as fine wine for a reason. I equate age with sensibility and a certain level of panache when wooing a woman, but it all depends on taste and what a person wants at the end of the day."

"In other words, younger men are useless to you," Dora concluded, chuckling when Sifon sighed in exasperation.

"Whatever, you'll never get it," she muttered, looking at the finely dressed people at the pool party she'd have wanted to avoid except Joshua; her business partner, and Dora's boyfriend, had booked rooms at the exquisite Manny Resort.

"I'm just teasing, Sifon, I get it. I might have been shocked three years ago when you first confessed your preference, but I've gotten used to it. I still believe you prefer them oldies because you've only been exposed to stupid younger guys. Besides, since you came out as a silver fox lover, I've never seen you with one. Sometimes, I'm tempted to assume you said that so that I would stop hooking you up on blind dates with gorgeous young men. You need to find one oldie soon, or we'll be back to hooking you up. I have a whole line-up of gorgeous, eager, young guys, even you won't be able to resist."

Sifon was left staring at her friend with open-mouthed amazement. She knew Dora could carry on a conversation with herself for hours but each time she experienced it, amazement was still part of her reaction.

"You done?"

Dora giggled into her wine glass. "I'm sorry for going on and on. I'm just really eager for you to date. I don't understand how you exist without the kind of happiness Joshua gives me as a boyfriend."

"Okay, no more drinks for you," Sifon said in exasperation, pulling the almost empty bottle of white wine to herself. Dora was a lightweight, and she had the propensity to talk more than usual when she was tipsy.

"Good idea," she burped, giggling while flailing her hands in front of her face, as though waving off an offensive smell.

Sifon shook her head with a smile and caught the eye of a waiter, waving him over to order a cold bottle of water for her friend. It wouldn't do for Dora to be sloshed by the time Joshua was ready to get down on one knee.

"It's a good thing Joshua got us a table. I don't envy these girls standing in high heels," Dora grimaced, looking at the crowd around the pool.

At least, she wasn't slurring. "Speaking of Joshua, where is he? He asked me not to leave early tomorrow as he wanted me to meet some sort of investor for breakfast."

Dora frowned at her. "Why would you want to leave early tomorrow? It's Sunday. Or, are you going to church?"

"That's all you got from that question, eh, Dora? Even though I'm not going to church, I need to prepare for Monday. Besides, I would've gone to church if your boyfriend hadn't booked rooms at this awesome resort just to celebrate his birthday."

Dora grinned, "He's a giver."

Sifon chuckled despite rolling her eyes at how happy her friend was with her man. "I agree."

"Even more so in bed. He..."

"TMI, Dora," Sifon interrupted without even looking at her friend. Her peripheral vision caught her pushing out her tongue. "I can still see you."

"Jeez, Sifon. I know you're older by just two years, but sometimes, you're as cool and collected as my mother, like you seem to know everything," she grumbled in the adorable manner that usually got Sifon smiling.

"And this is good, yes?"

Dora sniffed with her nose in the air. "Sometimes."

"I'll take that," she said, smiling when Dora scoffed.

The waiter arrived with the bottle of water and Sifon didn't have to prod Dora to drink; her eyes looked sharper after she returned from the bathroom a few minutes later.

"Thanks for the water."

"Thank your boyfriend, he's paying for it."

"But seriously though, Sifon, promise you will keep the questions to a minimum when I arrange another date for you. Utitofon complained that the date felt like he was sitting before his aunt. You even asked why he thought keeping that much beard was a good idea."

Sifon looked away from Dora's accusing gaze and shrugged. "Not everybody should keep a beard."

"That's all you have to say? Was it really necessary to school him on his choice of clothing?"

"The colour and style didn't fit his skin tone and persona."

Dora flung her hands in the air. "You have answers for everything."

Sifon grinned but then she felt it slip, her mouth going slack as her eyes came in contact with the most viscerally handsome man she'd ever seen. Of course, she'd seen handsome men before, but none had made her want to give up her innate maturity, a quality her mother had confessed had been a bit scary in a three-year-old.

She wanted to behave like girls less her age at the sight of a celebrity, and doing that would entail giggling like the girls who currently surrounded the stately man, who managed to exude class dressed in ragged blue jeans and a soft, white T-shirt which draped alluringly over his wide chest. His hat was cocked on his head at a jaunty angle, and his beard was neatly trimmed and dotted with white.

She sat up, her mouth still open in awe.

"No, I don't know everything," she said, thinking in her mind that she'd have known who the breathtaking, chocolate-complexioned man was if she knew everything. Her breathy response must have caught Dora's attention because her head swivelled to her, and she leaned close.

"Are you okay, Sifon?"

"Never been better. Who is that, though?" She was glad she'd decided to wear her contacts at the last minute. She might have missed this fantastic sight if she hadn't.

Dora followed her gaze. "You mean the man covered in girls?"

"They don't deserve him," she blurted out, shocking herself at how fierce she sounded.

Dora sat straighter. "Err...who are you, and what have you done with my 'cool, collected, and classy, no matter what' friend?"

She ignored Dora; her eyes fixed on the man, his poise, his height. He had on sneakers. He was dressed in a manner that Sifon would've abhorred if it was on a man her age. She couldn't explain why she was salivating at the sight of this man who shouldn't look so good in street clothes but did.

Despite seeming nice to the girls clinging to him, he looked aloof, while his arm rounded the waist of one of the scantily dressed girls angling for a selfie with him. Sifon gasped when she saw it.

"Well, if you must know. That's Joshua's mentor slash uncle, maybe even a pseudo father with how close they are. He owns this hotel and several others I've refused to be aware of. The man is wealthy as sin and..."

"...married." Sifon sounded so distraught that Dora's concerned mien didn't shock her.

CHAPTER TWO

"Well, men his age usually are," Dora pointed out.

She gulped her drink, filled her glass, and gulped that one down then filled her glass again.

"Sifon Akpan Alexander, stop what you're doing this minute!"

"Now who sounds like a mom?" Sifon muttered, but she held the full glass instead of gulping it down.

"You're scaring me."

I am scared, she thought, to be feeling this viscerally attracted to a man on sight. Now she was tempted to believe her aunty who swore that she had spiritual issues, the type acquired because one was connected to sea nymphs and water spirits.

Because why the hell was she not attracted to men her age? Why the hell didn't she feel anything, not even just raw sexual feelings for any of the guys who'd been giving her the eye all evening?

She had met Joshua first, a tall, broad-shouldered and nauseatingly handsome guy who'd been interested in her — had tried several times to take her out, but she'd refused because she'd not wanted to lead him on. Her aunty, her mom's sister, had been ready to cut off her head for rejecting the prime man.

Then she'd finally agreed to go out, on one condition; she was coming with her best friend. And she was glad Dora had been available as Joshua had been smitten on sight. He had been afraid and embarrassed to fall for Dora when he'd been trying to date her, but Sifon had been glad to set up her friend so that Joshua could talk to her.

And the rest is history. A year later, Joshua was about to propose to Dora. Aunty Felicia would kill her when she heard. And here she was, having all the feelings — pounding heart, belly butterflies and melting panties — for a married older man. She did have spiritual issues; it was the only explanation.

Sucking in a deep breath, she dropped her drink on the table and chuckled at Dora's confused look. "I'm fine. Na wa o, you too dey fear," she joked in pidgin English.

Dora sighed in obvious relief. "Good. Because this oldie lover thing is beginning to freak me out. That man is fine, but he—"

"Hey, baby," Joshua greeted, appearing beside Dora and swooping down to claim her lips right before her.

Sifon cleared her throat loudly. "Show some decorum, guys," she said, looking away with a smile when Dora moaned instead of heeding her comment.

Her eyes caught the sexy older man staring with a frown at Joshua, and as though he knew he was being observed, his eyes flicked to hers and held. Her heart plummeted into her stomach and bopped up again, almost lodging in her throat.

It must have been seconds that his narrowed eyes had been on her, but it felt like her whole life had flashed before her eyes in that moment. When he looked away, quite casually, as though she wasn't worth his time, Sifon rubbed her palms on her arms to cool them; in fact, her whole body was on a slow burn, and she wished she could hurry off into a shower before Joshua surprised Dora.

But that wasn't to be. Not when the DJ changed the music, and Joshua helped Dora from her seat, pulling her to the makeshift dance floor in front of the DJ's station.

Sifon sighed and pulled out her phone. This was it. She was super ecstatic for her friend, but she was also ready to call it a night.

***

Manny had always told Joshua, albeit as a joke, that he would probably be late for his own funeral. Having a past where his very breath had hinged on perfect timing, Manny respected time even in his presently relaxed lifestyle.

When Joshua's father, Manny's mentor, had died, leaving a twenty-year-old Joshua, he'd been devastated. The only wish Etuk had openly expressed in their covert dealings had been his unwillingness for Joshua to be introduced to that life.

And so, with nobody to look out for Joshua and a tendency for the headstrong boy to fall into a worse life than his father had lived, Manny had pulled out and dedicated his time to guiding Joshua right. And that meant he had to live a sparkling brand-new life free of the dark tentacles of the past. To the annoyance of many, he inundated that life with successful, legal businesses.

Twelve years later, he could pat himself on the back at having done well. He was sure Etuk would be happy with him wherever he was. Manny struggled with a bittersweet feeling as Joshua was getting engaged, bitter because his best friend was leaving, but sweet because he'd succeeded at fathering, something no one had believed he could do, even himself.

Joshua hadn't just been his friend but also his buffer from clingy women. So, when he'd arrived at the party with Joshua's assurance that he'd be waiting, he wasn't surprised he'd lied, but he was angry because the loose women who seemed to never be absent at parties in his hotel immediately attached themselves to his side like bees to honey.

At fifty-one, Manny was satisfied with how his life had turned out. He was sated with his successes; most important of all, Joshua, who had become like a son to him. With him getting engaged to be married soon, Manny was looking forward to the babies.

These days, he enjoyed sitting back to monitor his investments. He didn't want a woman at this point in his life, not after feeling the sting of betrayal from the fairer sex. Irene, his widowed same-age companion, could've been here. She made a better buffer from these young girls than Joshua, but she wasn't answering his calls because he'd been honest and told her that there were absolutely no strings attached to their copulating. She was miffed that he was unwilling to repeat the stroll down the aisle, but once was enough.

"Manny," one of the many girls squealed, giggling as she jumped in place, causing Manny to worry for her safety as she balanced on heels she had no business wearing by the slippery poolside.

He smiled the fake smile he reserved for such crowds and once again confirmed that the present generation lacked basic self-preservation skills.

"Can I get a selfie, please?"

With superhuman effort employed to control his urge to roll his eyes or snap at these females who couldn't read simple body language, since he'd been exuding that he wanted to be alone, he shrugged, his left hand rounding her bare waist as he grimaced at the phone camera for the selfie shot.

Where the hell was Joshua?

While he pulled out his phone to chat the young man up, his skin prickled; someone was watching him. To a person without the experience of his past, they'd scoff and point out that the poolside was littered with people staring at everybody. But Manny knew better.

The prickling had tickled the back of his neck the moment he'd walked up to the bustling poolside of his hotel. He'd scanned the area while pretending to be busy with the clingy girls but had found nothing. Now, standing aside to text Joshua, his skin felt like it crawled with insects.

Manny: Where the hell are you, boy?

Josh: Here!

At his instant reply, Manny looked up, scanned, and finally found Joshua already tongue-deep in his girlfriend's mouth. He smirked at his antics while some catcalls erupted, but a frown remained as he scanned for...

His heart lurched when his gaze caught larger, feminine eyes that stared at him as though he'd hung the moon, eliciting an instant, strange feeling in him to actually want to hang the moon.

Yeah, not happening, he thought, and looked away, maintaining a stoic expression as though his blood-pumping organ wasn't pounding a staccato against his chest and his neck didn't ache with the need to find those eyes again.

With a frown, Manny narrowed his eyes, an effort to focus on Joshua and not give into the strange pull... Oh, breath was knocked out of him when she stood and followed Joshua and Dora to the dance floor, her phone out and filming.

Sweet heavens! Manny had to shut his mouth when a cool breeze grazed his tongue. He'd not even realized his mouth had dropped, but he couldn't be angry, not when she deserved slack-jawed admiration.

She was young, that much was obvious from her face, even though the light illuminating the pool area didn't reveal a lot. But brilliance wasn't needed to see the clear silhouette of her very curvy body. Spit dried up in his mouth. He'd never had this sort of reaction to a woman before, and while he couldn't look away, he reminded himself of his self-imposed fast from women after Irene.

Ogling her almost made Manny miss Joshua's moment, but it was her wide, absolutely breathtaking smile that made him seek the reason for her happiness. It turned out Joshua had gone down on one knee, and Dora was screaming like a banshee. That girl was a handful, and his Joshua was head over heels in love with her, which meant he loved her too.

Applause and catcalls erupted and music played while Dora's squeals floated over the noise as she hung off Joshua's broad shoulders in a tight hug, both her high-heeled feet off the floor and bent upward while Joshua held on and twirled with her.

He clapped with the crowd but his eyes swept to the strange siren, tracking her body and landing at her feet to check if she had on heels. Why he did that was anybody's guess, because he couldn't explain the act, either. Manny only knew that finding her in flat, beaded sandals, his gaze roving over her loose from the knees and tight at the hip and arse pants, floaty chiffon top, light enough to reveal the tight, black, sleeveless camisole beneath which emphasized the soft-looking weight of her breasts...gave him a curious kind of joy, one he still couldn't explain.

In the sea of skinny, scantily-dressed females, her plump, covered body stood out — not like a sore thumb, but a fat, fresh, ripe finger of plantain in the midst of so many unripe fingers. He loved ripe plantain, go figure that he would describe her as his favourite food; did that mean he liked her?

Scoffing, he shook his head, vehemently denying the thought and determinedly looking away. Enough of the nonsense, he was here for Joshua and Dora. Women would always be mere play things to him, with their helplessly deceitful nature.

Manny smiled, having succeeded in demeaning the strange feeling he'd gotten from sighting the strange woman. He moved towards Joshua and his betrothed with genuine happiness.

"My boy," he hugged Joshua, slapping his back a couple of times. "I'm really proud of you."

Joshua grinned and hugged him tight, his joy effusive. Dora wasn't far off; Manny hugged the spry lady, chuckling at her inability to stop squealing.

He couldn't explain how it happened. With the deluge of Joshua's friends converging on him to offer their congratulations, he made sure he stood aside to avoid being jostled. It was for naught, as he still got jostled so bad that his hat flew off his head.

Growling his detest, he turned a frown to the culprit, and those large eyes triggered shocks all over his body, especially burning where her body had brushed his. The instant reaction angered him; he didn't want to be feeling this way, not at this age, so he snapped.

"Watch where you're going! No need to trample the rest of us with your clumsiness."

He instantly regretted his words when hurt flashed in her eyes. She murmured her apology, biting her plump lips as she looked away. As though she couldn't bear sharing the same air space with him, she shoved through the enthusiastic young men that must have jostled her in the first place.

An unconscious growl escaped his throat when the young guys excused her but touched her back with the excuse of helping her through the throng of people, their perusing eyes immediately dropping to her impressive arse when she walked by.

What the hell was the matter with him?

Manny picked up his hat and stalked towards the bar. He ordered a whisky, and while he waited for it to be poured, his eyes unconsciously tracked the gathering, specifically, the area she had been headed.

He wasn't disappointed, except at himself. He watched her speak to Dora, a wide happy smile on her face. She hugged Dora, and just before she walked away, obviously leaving the party, he glimpsed forlornness in her gaze. Manny felt both guilty and relieved; guilty because he felt responsible for her pain at his unnecessary callousness, and relieved because he was sure he'd never see her again.

CHAPTER THREE

Sifon still felt groggy, despite the just concluded hot then cold bath she'd taken. Nothing changed as she sat on the luxurious hotel bed with the cool blast of the AC rapidly drying up the water on her skin while she rummaged in her bag for lotion. Her head felt heavy while her eyes were grainy as though she'd barely slept.

It was Joshua's fault for being such a giver; he had left a bottle of Lambrusco wine in her mini fridge and an SMS to make sure she got it. She'd scoffed and readied for bed but couldn't sleep, no matter how much she tried. How could she, when she was equal parts embarrassed, hurt, and damn horny from meeting Mr. Sexy Ogre?

She groaned every time she recalled his words — the number one reason she'd been unable to sleep, until she'd attacked the wine and had finally fallen into uneasy slumber. It was supposed to be an escape from the hurtful words which became a loop in her mind, but her subconscious replayed the damn scene in her dreams; it was no wonder she woke up tired.

Watch where you're going! No need to trample the rest of us with your clumsiness.

They were callous words, and she was embarrassed that she might have let her pain show; but nothing could explain why she was obsessing about the gravelly nature of his voice and how it had, despite the loud music, travelled through her body like a freight train.

Could he have been invariably pointing out her weight with his choice of the words, 'trample' and 'clumsiness'? With an exasperated sigh, Sifon concluded the man was an arsehole.

She dressed up with jerky movements while erasing from her mind someone she wasn't going to meet again. She needed to clear her mind of both him and the tiredness he'd caused and get prepared for the meeting Joshua had slated for 8:30 a.m.

Standing before the full-length mirror, she surveyed herself, turning sideways to scrutinize her curves. Her breasts were an okay size, but compared to her behind, they ended up looking small. For her 5'6" height, her arse was eye-bulgingly obvious and often a cause for personal embarrassment for her. People, guys mostly, saw the arse and assumed she was down for casual sex. She had no idea where that stupid notion emanated from, but she'd long since learnt how to handle men who saw her as a sex object instead of a brilliant businesswoman.

Sifon sighed. It was tiring at times, though, to always have to prove herself. Every day, since she first began noticing how boys and men stared at her, she'd wished some of the bulk of her arse would magically transfer to her boobs, balancing everything; but alas, those things only happened in movies. Her mom had chuckled and said it was the curse of the Amah family; all the women had large behinds. Her mother had had it, and Aunty Felicia had it, too.

Her overnight luggage was zipped at 7:50 a.m.; the plan was to dump the luggage in her car then search out Manny Resort's dining room to wait for Joshua and the prospective investor. She was about to leave the room when the bedside telephone rang.

It was the reception calling to inform her of a reserved table at the dining room by one Mr. Joshua

Etuk. Right, nothing was amiss with that, except why was he reserving the table for her?

Sifon sighed, shook off the worry and left the room. It always only took a little while for any of her business partner's plans to unfold, no matter how confusing they seemed at the onset. After running their haulage company together for three years, she knew him, and he knew her, and they were ready to expand, ergo, the meeting with this investor and various others during the month.

After dropping off her room key at the reception and her luggage in her car, a porter directed her to the dining room which could double as a conference hall. Maybe it does, Sifon thought, shutting her mouth and smiling at the waiter who welcomed her.

"I'm told I have a reserved table," she commented after the pleasantries.

"Name, please."

"Sifon Alex."

He smiled, "Right this way, Ma," and led her to a table by a huge bay window.

The room carried small round tables covered in white with four seats. Sunlight streamed through the drawn light yellow cotton blinds on the windows, magnifying the beauty of the setting.

"Thank you," she said, smiling at the waiter who had solicitously dragged out a seat for her. When he didn't leave immediately after she'd sat, she looked up with a raised eyebrow and caught him signalling to his colleague, a blur at a distance, who arrived with a tea tray.

They quietly and efficiently arranged the spread before her while she dug in her purse for her phone.

"May I pour your hot water?"

"Please." Sifon cleared her throat in a bid to curb her humour.

"We were informed that you have your own special tea?" the waiter who'd welcomed her asked.

He was really handsome, maybe about her age. Someone she should be falling for, but she felt absolutely nothing. Nodding to his question, she said, "I do, thank you, very much."

"My pleasure. I'll be back in ten minutes in case you need something else."

And he was gone before she could respond that she'd not need anything else. With an exasperated sigh, she rummaged in her purse, brought out a pack of her green tea and had to pull out her Samsung pad before finding the smaller Android phone. She knew exactly what Joshua was up to, and she needed to make him aware of her knowledge.

***

"I'm told I have a reserved table."

Innocent words, but said in a sultry tone that sent goose bumps spreading along his forearms and his head jerking up to identify the owner of the voice. Manny barely controlled the unconscious gasp that almost became a cough, but he pinched his nose and breathed through his mouth until the need to wrack passed.

What the hell was she doing here?

He wondered this while his gaze eagerly ate up the sight of her luscious figure in Ankara shorts worn beneath a baggy white T-shirt, which did nothing to hide her generous endowments.

As Manny sat on the other side of the entrance, he knew she'd not seen him, but he could see all of her. She had no make-up on, her braids were in a top-bun, and she had on fluffy flip-flops. He had never seen any young woman so casually dressed, at least, not the ones that frequented his hotel. Those ones were always decked out and ready to impress as his hotel housed the crème de la crème of society.

He watched her walk behind the waiter, her rear view a beautiful sight. Manny scoffed at himself, feeling like a dirty old man, and looked down at his cup of coffee. A second later, he looked up at her again as he couldn't control the urge.

A growl lodged in his throat, his jaw tightening as he watched the waiter, a handsome, tall, young guy, drag out her seat and pay unflinching attention to her. He hated that she smiled at him. He hated the waiter's attention on her, blithely ignoring the fact that he was just doing his job and he seemed quite good at it.

Shaking his head to clear the strange fog that came with being in the same environment with the woman, Manny grabbed his cup and sipped his coffee. It did nothing to wipe away the inquisitiveness that plagued him. He was inundated with the need to go to her table and ask, in the rudest manner, who the hell she was and why she was in his head.

Quite ridiculous, Manny thought, but maybe it would cure him of this infatuation. He would be, at least, twenty-five years older than her, and he'd never gone that young before.

Why was he even contemplating being with her?

"Jesus," he murmured, rubbing his face and watching as she pulled a teabag from the pack she'd removed from her bag and dunked it in her cup of hot water. Weird that she moved about with her own tea.

With determination, he looked away from her and tapped his phone to read the day's paper online. He was almost congratulating himself that he'd succeeded in ignoring her when the handsome waiter approached her again, this time carrying a big glass mug, filled to the brim with...ice cream, this early?

"Your parfait, Ma," he offered, flashing her a smile which she returned while shaking her head as though confused as to why she was receiving the delicacy.

Parfait wasn't part of the menu. Manny was about to call the waiter when her voice carried in the near empty dining room as she made a call...to her boyfriend, perhaps. Anger bloomed in his chest for no reason.

"I know this is a bribe. You plan to show up late, right?" Humour laced her tone; she wasn't angry that her companion was going to show up late.

"How long will you be?" Manny shook his head. If he was meeting this woman, he'd be waiting for her, not the other way around. Not that he wanted anything to do with her. To prove this, he looked at his phone, noticing a message from Joshua sent a couple of minutes earlier. He would, of course, be running late and asked for pardon, that damn boy.

She giggled. Manny had experienced women giggling before, but never had it filled his heart with brightly coloured bubbles...it made his heart light, like everything was alright with the world.

"Whatever," she said, before clicking off the call and pulling the glass mug close.

He was just shaking off the light-hearted feeling when she moaned in obvious ecstasy after taking a scoop of her treat. He heard her clearly. She sat two tables and a door from him, but he heard her, his whole body heard her.

It was unconscious, no doubt; he knew this because her head came up and looked around, as though checking to find if anybody had heard her. She looked over her shoulder and he quickly ducked his gaze, not sure if she caught him staring. When he peeked at her again, she was head down and enjoying her Greek yogurt mix.

Manny was grateful that it was a Sunday; most guests weren't up at this time, and if they were, they'd be ordering breakfast in their rooms. He was also grateful that he'd dressed in a native jumper, the top long enough to cover the effect her moan had on his lower body.

With anger at his susceptibility, he shoved from his seat and marched towards the kitchen to see the head cook.

"Good morning, Sir," the middle-aged man sputtered, shocked to find him in the kitchen that early. The cook was about his age but had lived a sedentary life for too long, and it showed in the bulge hanging over his belt.

Whereas, Manny had lived a life too active if compared to the average fellow. Even after retiring from that life, it'd become a habit to work out; with that, his energy level was way higher than that of most young people. He'd maintained his physique; only his experience, weathered looks, and grey hairs alerted his age.

"I didn't know we'd added parfait to the menu."

The cook looked flummoxed. "We...we didn't, Sir."

Why not?

Manny took a deep breath to disperse that foreign thought. "But a lady out there is having one."

"Oh, err...one of the rooms ordered it and requested the kitchen receive it and present it to the...err, lady." The cook seemed worried that he might have done something wrong. The practice was not foreign, but neither was it often performed.

Manny's lips twitched to ask which room had ordered the yogurt, but he shook off the thought when he realized it was of no use, especially since he had nothing and would have nothing to do with her. There was no need behaving like a jealous spouse.

"Where was it ordered from?" Now he was thinking business. Truth be told, if parfait gave her that much enjoyment, then he needed to have it on his menu. He convinced himself that it wasn't for her, but for added value and pleasure to his guests.

"Blaize Foods, Sir."

"Do I know them?" he frowned, then decided it didn't matter. "Don't worry, just have the manager meet with them and negotiate the availability of parfait at the resort."

"Of course, Sir."

Manny nodded and turned to leave but heard the cook choke, as though about to say something.

"Yes?" Manny prodded, noticing the cook's discomfort. When his eyes scanned the large, fully equipped industrial kitchen, he noticed how conspicuously attentive the other kitchen staff were to their duties. They had the stiffened stance of people trying hard to show they weren't listening or interested in the ongoing conversation.

"Err..."

"Is there a problem, Mr. Marcus?"

"We just wanted to wish you a fine Sunday, Sir. And we really appreciate how good you are to us."

Manny wasn't buying it, but he played along. "I'm honoured, Mr. Marcus. And you people make it easy to be a good boss, you're all good staff. Have a nice day, all of you." He nodded and walked out. When the door banged behind him, furious whispers erupted, but he couldn't make out what they were saying.

"Oh, there you are. Good morning, Uncle."

Joshua turned the corner, grinning — his go-to attitude when he once again turned up late for a meeting. Manny didn't want to dwell on the over-flogged issue, so he raised his eyebrow and looked over Joshua's broad shoulder, as though searching for someone.

"Uncle? Where's your silent partner? I am eager to meet this enigma." He rolled his eyes in sarcasm and hugged the young man who chuckled over his shoulder.

"She's your kind of person, keeps to time to a fault. She's been in the dining room for a while," he said, walking with him down the corridor that led to the dining room.

"Not a long while, because I just left the dining less than three minutes ago."

Joshua stopped at the retractable door with the glassy top. The dining room could be observed from behind the door without having to open it.

"There she is." Joshua pointed and stood aside for him to look. He wasn't as tall as Joshua, but he could easily look through the glass without tiptoeing.

Only the strange woman sat in the dining room, still. Though his heart stumbled at the sight of her, he ignored it and frowned, "I don't see anyone." He turned to Joshua.

The young man stood behind him. "That's her. That's Sifon, my partner."

"Her?"

"Uh...Manny, what's the problem? You know her?" Joshua's brow furrowed.

"She looks like...you do know women are generally deceitful, right? What the hell does she have to offer as a business partner?" Even as he said the words, he mentally cringed, imagining how hurt she'd be if she heard him; probably more than she'd been by the pool last night, a look he couldn't seem to forget.

"Uh, only a whole lot! The success of my company, our company, that you see, is mostly her."

Manny shrugged. "She certainly has a lot of flesh to spread around."

Joshua's eyes widened at his insinuation, his hands rising to his head. "Jesus, uncle Manny, I'm thinking we should reschedule this meeting. Wait, did Aunty Irene call?"

"Call? She hasn't picked my calls in months. Why do you ask?" Now he was angry with himself.

"Well, you're only this mean and callous when you guys quarrel and she reminds you of your dead wife."

"Dead ex-wife," he corrected. "And enough with the Uncle; what are you, five?"

"Whatever, I don't want you to be like this with Sifon. She's a good person, the best partner I could ever ask for."

Manny narrowed his eyes at him. "Are you sleeping with her?" The thought got him so furious, a red haze covered his gaze, and he took a threatening step closer to Joshua. "You're engaged, young man, you shouldn't be messing around with—"

"Whoa, whoa, whoa! Uncle...Manny." Joshua had both hands raised in front of him. "First of all, I am hurt that you think I'd cheat on Dora and then have the effrontery to say it to your face. Second, Sifon isn't that kind of person. I met her years before Dora..."

"So, she's an old fling?" he spat and wondered how Joshua wasn't seeing what a jealous boar he'd become.

"Jesus, no! I met her years before I met Dora, and in all that time, she rejected my advances as though I had fleas or something."

Manny sighed in relief, one he didn't understand as he continued to face off with his ward.

"We met at a job interview, we both got the job and had to work together. She's very beautiful and so fucking intelligent, so I went after her, but she refused. And in more and more of our conversations, the idea came to start the company. She was responsible for the first three big clients we landed due to her excellent negotiation skills and plain determination. After over two years, she agreed to go on a date with me, but only in the company of her best friend, Dora, who I ended up falling in love with...and I'm marrying," Joshua added in exasperation.

Steam left his sails, and he looked through the glass again at her... Sifon. Putting a name to her made her more memorable and difficult to erase. She had on earphones, connected to the pad which she'd positioned in front of her glass mug while she nibbled on her parfait; she leaned so close, seemingly fascinated by what was on the screen. "Probably watching Netflix or ROK on her little pad," he sneered, thinking aloud.

If someone asked him why he was being so unflattering about Sifon, he wouldn't know what to answer. He didn't understand it. Yet, even as Joshua levelled him with a look that could kill, he still had to say more; he was a drowning man searching for a hold to save himself.

"I am close to insulting you, Uncle. So close," Joshua said, pushing the door so forcefully its retraction almost smashed Manny's face.

He felt ashamed but followed his ward anyway. He had to make sure he would not be doing business with Sifon, which meant he'd not be doing business with Joshua. He could just recommend their company to some of his associates. All he needed was to never be in close proximity with her.

"Hey there, love!" Joshua bent behind Sifon, holding her shoulders in a form of greeting while looking at her screen. "What are you watching?"

Sifon flashed him a smile over her shoulder, pulling out her earphones. "What do you think?"

"Oh, wow, look at that, CNN. I'm shocked," Joshua said in mock sarcasm, straightening to give Manny the stink eye, an expression that Sifon didn't notice because he remained behind her seat.

"You managed to make it on time," Sifon chuckled. She turned in her seat and squinted at her partner, then her smile blanched. Manny couldn't blame her, not after what he'd said last night.

"Why are you not wearing your contacts or glasses?" Joshua asked, picking the seat beside her and allowing Manny to make his choice of seat.

Manny pressed his lips together, not in anger that his ward was openly being impolite by not introducing them before taking a seat, but because he was controlling himself from blurting out his concern for her sight. Guilt chewed at him as he realized she'd leaned close and seemed fascinated at her screen because she was short-sighted.

"Err..." She clicked off her pad and made a show of flipping over the cover before she replied. "That's your fault."

"My fault...how?" Joshua looked confused, even though he had on a smile.

Manny pinned his ward with an accusing look then had to breathe deep to calm himself and not be so obvious. The plan was to never see her again, not to become her champion.

Sifon looked up with a knowing gaze for Joshua and a small smile. Manny wished she'd directed the smile and luminous gaze at him rather than the scared look he'd gotten earlier.

"The wine, my eyes feel grainy," she smiled, and as though she'd heard his earlier thought, the smile remained as she turned to him. "Good morning. Care to join us?" Because she had probably been wondering why he just stood there, staring at her like a lost child.

Manny cleared his throat, embarrassment burning in his chest. "Thank you," he managed and sat opposite her.

Joshua's gaze was still full of anger, but he sighed and smiled at Sifon. "So, Sifon, this is my uncle, who's more like a father to me, Mr. Manuel Ekpe, but we all just call him Manny."

"Manny, this is my friend and partner, Sifon Alex, we co-own the haulage business."

Sifon turned her full gaze on him. Her eyes softened with her smile. Clearly, she'd decided to forego his rudeness the previous night. While Joshua introduced him to her, she'd stared at him like she'd done from across the pool, and then she'd gone and bit her plump lower lip, as though she couldn't control her reaction to the sight of him, a reaction that he plainly felt like a hot breeze against his face as their gazes held.

"It's a pleasure... Sir."

Her husky voice triggered images of tangled limbs on sultry nights. Manny wanted to swallow her voice, her lips, all of her, and that wasn't good. He didn't want to feel this way. Feeling this way always led to strings and commitments, and he definitely didn't want that, especially not with someone so young. It didn't matter what Joshua would think of him, he needed to nip this breathless connection in the bud.

Manny levelled her with a cool gaze. "Is it?"

CHAPTER FOUR

The meeting had become a complete disaster three minutes in; Sifon had gotten the impression that Manny wanted nothing to do with their company. It was a skill she'd had to develop in their first year of running the company, knowing when a customer or investor was really interested and not just paying them lip service.

Despite her heart-thumping attraction to him, Sifon had noticed that Joshua's uncle or mentor slash guardian was desperate in his attempts to belittle the efforts of their company. She had stopped trying to convince him and had let Joshua, who'd become clearly furious, keep talking.

It had lasted less than ten minutes, and despite Manny's glaring attempt at sabotage, Sifon had smiled and repeated the sentiment — it's been a pleasure.

"I'm so sorry, Sifon, I don't know what's come over him. He's been curious about the company since its inception, but you know this was something I wanted to do without his help, and you've been my divine partner who he's been adamant to meet. But...today... I really don't understand what happened," Joshua heaved, his face scrunched in a deep frown.

While he spoke, Sifon nodded, unlocking her car. She flung her handbag onto the passenger seat and proceeded to twist the handle on her car door that would bring down the glass. She bit her lip while putting in effort to wind down the glass with the hope that it would lessen the pain that Manny being a certified arsehole had settled in her chest.

"It's fine, Joshua." She blew out a breath when she was done. She wiped perspiration from her temple while squinting up at him. "We have other investors to meet." Maybe it was a good thing that he didn't want to invest in their company; with the way she was feeling, emotions could interfere with business decisions, and she didn't want that. Perhaps, his bad attitude would help curb the intense emotions she had for him.

"Out of all of them, apart from my uncle, we were only sure of one other guy, Udeko, and I don't like him."

Sifon nodded. "We can only try. We've been surprised before, maybe one or two of the ones we weren't sure of will come through," she shrugged, smiling at Joshua to relieve his worry. She knew he was feeling guilty and embarrassed at how his uncle had acted with her. She didn't understand it, either. He'd acted as though she might have offended him before; could it be from jostling him last night? That was hardly her fault and not something to cause a lifelong rift.

"How the hell are you still calm and smiling after what he did in there?"

"He has his reasons, Joshua. We've been known to reject offers on sight because we weren't...comfortable with the person offering it." She looked away to hide the hurt that was sure to show in her eyes and fiddled with the torn upholstery on her car door.

Joshua scoffed, his fury palpable in the disbelieving shake of his head. Then he took a deep breath and focused on her. "You really should get a new car."

"And that is my cue to get out of here. See you tomorrow, Joshua. And hug my friend for me." She slid into her car and Joshua shut the door for her.

"I will. I know you've said the car...makes you feel closer to your mom, but..."

"It would be like abandoning her memory if I get a new car."

"Jesus, Sifon, you loved your mom. Even when we met, you were always speaking about something she did; I was shocked to find out she was late. You will never forget her, she's always in your heart."

Sifon groaned. "Stop sounding so reasonable." She turned the ignition, and the car sputtered and died.

"See what I mean? I'm afraid the car will die on you at a very inopportune time, maybe in the middle of nowhere on a cold, scary night."

"Stop!"

Joshua chuckled, "You're so easy to scare. I wish Dora was more like that."

Sifon shook her head. "You deserve each other." She tried again and whooped in victory when the car revved. She wasted no time in reversing from the lot. "Don't be too hard on your uncle," she advised when she'd completed her reverse.

"See you on Monday, Sisi," he responded instead, totally avoiding what she'd said because he was obviously planning to be hard on the man.

She chuckled, shaking her head and leaning on the steering wheel to look at him through the window. "We don't force people into business, Joshua. They have to believe in it, or else it defeats the purpose of partnering with them in the first place."

"Yes, mom."

Sifon shook her head and drove off, tapping her horn as she made the turn towards the gate.

***

It was a gaffe of debilitating proportions. Manny couldn't believe he'd messed up so unforgivably.

How could a woman...a young woman, have made him so jittery he'd acted like a teenager? He'd seen, met, and been with so many women, sophisticated and otherwise, so it shouldn't have been an issue. He should have listened critically to their plans and asked sensible questions about their profit margins and projections, not become petty and judgemental.

It didn't help that she'd been so calm, he'd ended up feeling like the younger person in her presence. And she'd been polite to the end, never deserving of his snide remarks.

He paced the length of his office, knowing that Joshua was on his way to bite off his head, and he deserved it. He deserved every harangue his ward would give him, but after that, what then?

Would he do business with them, which would entail being in close proximity with Sifon? His heart leaped at the thought and equally squeezed in trepidation. Or, would he restrict dealings to Joshua alone?

Manny shook his head; the Joshua he knew was vindictive and would require as his penance that he apologise and deal with Sifon directly. From all their conversations about the company, he'd had a lot of good to say about his partner and had been excited for both of them to meet.

"Ah, fuck," he muttered as he heard Joshua's stomps up the stairs. "Here we go."

"What the hell, uncle?" Joshua busted into the office in a huff.

"I am, truly, sorry," Manny said with all manner of sincerity.

"If I didn't know any better, or if we'd had other investors around, I'd think you were trying to sabotage our chances at growth." Joshua was heaving.

The palpability of his fury and his words made Manny flinch. "I'm so sorry, Joshua, believe me. I'm ashamed of myself right now," he sighed, rubbing his palm over his face.

Joshua paced the length of his office like he'd done a couple of minutes earlier with a furrowed brow. "What I don't understand is why? Why would you act that way with her? Because I sure know it wasn't about me." He pinned Manny with a scrutinizing look.

"Err..." Manny cleared his throat and tapped the back of his swivelling leather chair. This was the question he'd been afraid of; what was he to tell his ward?

"I'd expected you to act like a boar with Dora when I introduced her to you. I mean, she's trendy and looks more like a possible gold digger, if that's what you're worried about..."

"It's not—"

"But..." Joshua continued as though he'd not spoken, and Manny sighed, rubbed his eyes tiredly, and waited for the young man to finish his postulation. "You were nice to Dora until you'd studied her, and then you told me you liked her for me."

"Joshua, there's no need—"

"I expected you," he spoke over him again, "to love Sifon at first sight."

"What?" he sputtered, his heart beating a staccato. Did he know?

"I mean, she's your kind of person — always on time and cares about business. In fact, she's obsessed about business and success."

"Oh," Manny sighed in relief. He didn't know he was madly attracted to her, which had made him act the fool, but Joshua telling him these good things about her wasn't helping. Like knowing her name, it deepened these feelings he didn't want to have.

"Yeah, oh. You didn't give her a chance, and it makes me wonder, have you met her before?" Joshua's gaze was searching.

"Err..." He considered lying, but what more would that do than dig this hole he'd found himself in deeper? He scratched his right brow and sighed, "I met her last night."

Joshua's frown deepened. "I don't recall introducing you. I wanted both of you to meet the first time this morning."

"You didn't. She...bumped into me." Manny was uncomfortable with this conversation; he felt exposed.

"Was she rude? Didn't she apologize?" Joshua just really needed to know why he'd been uncouth with Sifon. Manny didn't blame him, his attitude needed explicit explanation.

"No, she wasn't rude, but I was... Joshua, see, I'm sorry, and I promise I'll make it up to you."

"To me? Hell no, uncle, you aren't getting off that easy. Since you don't want to tell me what the issue is, and you're feeling apologetic, then make it up to the person you deliberately offended for no reason — Sifon."

"But—"

Joshua pulled out his wallet, fished out a card and dropped it on his table. "There's her card. Call her and discuss what we should have discussed today. And do it soon, because you aren't the only investor we've planned to meet, and we need just one. I'm not speaking with you until Sifon tells me she's had a sit-down with you, and it better have positive results or we probably will never speak again."

"Joshua!"

The slam of his office door was the reply to his call. Manny shook his head, sighing and walking to his window. Joshua was as dramatic in anger as his dad had been. Etuk had usually kept his word, and Joshua was the same. Manny had no idea what to do. He still didn't want any strings with a woman, especially not Sifon, but his attraction to her was too strong to ignore.

CHAPTER FIVE

He sank his fingers into her hair, massaging her scalp, and it sent thrills gliding down her body. Just massaging her head made her nipples tingle and harden. It caused warmth to swirl in the pit of her stomach, and her thighs tightened and pressed together, a moan echoing in her mind as her toes curled on the bed.

Were his hands enchanted? She'd known there was something enthralling about Manny, and he was revealing it with this simple massage. What would it feel like when he got his hands on her body? Those hands that were causing havoc in her body by just being in her hair; she licked her lips when she imagined them on her bare breasts.

She moaned and scooted backwards, aligning her back to his front, and smiled when she felt the monstrous bulge in his trousers; he was affected, too — good, she thought. She pressed her buttocks to that mound, moaning as the warmth in her stomach boiled and leaked between her thighs, preparing her for more action that wouldn't require clothing.

"You like it?" His deep voice whispered directly to her, and it was as thrilling as tonguing the shell of her ear. She gasped and nodded.

"Do you want me to touch you here...and take your ache away?" He had his hand in her trousers, his finger already testing the wet heat that had pooled there. "Oh, Sifon...baby...the things I'll do to this..." He tapped her clit and dipped his finger into the wet heat. "Oh, my baby..."

She jerked and widened her thighs, her hips undulating, she was so close, and gasped, "Yes, daddy."

"Who's your daddy? Sifon, wake up!"

Joshua's voice broke through the sensual fog in her mind like the sudden pierce of a flashlight in a dark room. She groaned, squeezed her eyes and tried to return to the dream.

"How do you even squeeze yourself in that chair? It's a miracle that you fit in it sitting down, but curling up like a cat to sleep on it should be one of the world's wonders."

"Go away," she grumbled, trying to burrow into the seat that barely contained her. The chair had been her mother's favourite relaxing spot at home. It was a weirdly shaped chair; though it wasn't a couch, it was a bit bigger than a regular single seater. She'd moved it to her small office, another thing that made her feel closer to her mother. Her scent, though faint, lingered on the faded upholstery; it calmed her when she was stressed and lulled her to sleep on tired days.

"So, what's up with napping at the office these days? Aren't you sleeping well at night?"

You could say that, she thought, and it is all because of your sexy uncle who finds it fun to plague my mind and rob me of sleep. She sighed wearily as she straightened her bent legs in a stretch, yawning in the process. "Naps are refreshing."

"Uh huh, especially with your daddy," Joshua snickered, leaning his arse on her desk while he crossed his ankles, folded his arms, and pinned her with a knowing look.

Sifon sat up facing him and frowned, "What?"

"When I called, you said 'yes, daddy'," Joshua imitated a breathless tone.

Her heart stuttered; what else had he heard? Sifon set her facial expression to uncaring as she shrugged, "Uh huh, which would mean I was dreaming about my dad."

Joshua scoffed, "You don't even know your father."

"Stepdad, then," she snapped, wondering why he wouldn't just let it go; can't someone have a sensual dream in peace?

"The one you had a crush on? That would explain a lot," he grinned, his eyes twinkling in suppressed humour.

"Jesus, does Dora ever shut up?"

"Nope."

"I'm going to kill her, and for good measure, clog that leaking faucet of a mouth of hers." Sifon fell back on the chair while Joshua laughed, bending from the waist. She rolled her eyes. "I'm glad I could entertain you this afternoon."

"It's evening. You've been napping for a while." He chuckled at her widened eyes.

"Well, is there any particular reason you woke me up?" She narrowed her eyes at him and ended up smiling when she couldn't hold the tough look.

"You mean, apart from telling you it's past closing time?" Joshua grinned and then cleared his throat and looked serious. "You'll have to attend the Commissioner's dinner without me."

Sifon frowned, "Why?"

It wasn't that she couldn't attend the dratted event by herself or speak to the commissioner, which was the aim of attending, but she appreciated her partner's presence, having someone to refer snide remarks to and chuckle with behind hands while the probably boring event progressed.

"Dora's parents are in town."

"Oh, I thought that was tomorrow."

"Dora said her mom convinced her dad that there was no difference between today and tomorrow." Joshua sighed as though exasperated.

Sifon smiled. "Sounds like someone we know." She gave him a knowing look. "That'll be you in fifty years."

A loving smile appeared on his face with a far off gaze. "Yeah," he nodded and his gaze focused. "So, you're good to speak with the commissioner on your own?"

"You have to ask?" She eyed him and smiled. "What kind of dinner is it again?"

"His alumni association is giving him an award."

"And he's hosting it at his house? Shouldn't the alumni be responsible for that?"

Joshua shrugged in a 'what can you do' manner. "Big men; he probably offered to sponsor the event."

She nodded. "We need to get to that level soon."

"We will." Joshua stood and offered her his hands. She grabbed on, and he pulled her from the seat. "So, report tomorrow?"

Sifon eyed him. "I'm not stepping foot in this office tomorrow. I'm going to have a normal weekend for once this month," she griped.

Joshua scoffed, "As if you can have a normal weekend with your eccentric aunty. Anyway, I didn't mean a physical report. I meant a call, at least."

"Do not remind me of Aunty Felicia, let's hope she has church programs the whole of tomorrow." Sifon crossed her fingers as she rounded her desk to get her bag.

Joshua chuckled, "Why not wish for the whole weekend while you're at it?"

"Amen," she replied fervently. "Besides, Kay called earlier; he said the line-up at the granite depot might take days to get to our turn."

"So, ETA, at least, Monday?"

Sifon nodded and clicked off the socket feeding her TV and small refrigerator.

"You should practice switching off the TV before the socket."

She pinned him with a wide-eyed look. "I don't care," she enunciated.

Joshua shook his head and left her office while she crosschecked that her windows were locked. When she locked her door, which stood beside Joshua's own office, he was already at the little reception, speaking on the phone with Dora. She could hear the conversation from where she stood.

Their company office was small, and with the number of clients trickling in, they needed to upgrade, hence the need for investors. If they were going to branch off to other haulage material apart from the building materials they currently were into, they needed to look the part. They needed more trucks, more drivers, more administrative staff — they needed an investor.

By the time she checked everywhere to make sure the office was secure, Joshua was outside, still on the phone, the reflection of the setting sun glinting off his sleek SUV.

She locked up, got into her mother's beat-up Toyota Corolla which looked ugly beside Joshua's Highlander SUV, turned the ignition, and smiled in relief when it responded with one try. Sticking her tongue out at a chuckling Joshua, she waved and drove off, hoping she made it to the event on time.

***

As it happened, the dinner wasn't at the commissioner's house but the Guest House beside his home.

Sifon was impressed that their names were on the check-in list at the entrance of the hall where the event was already underway. No matter the urgency she'd expressed in getting here on time, it'd been close to difficult shaking off her aunty, who felt every time was the right time to bring up marriage issues.

An usher showed her to a round table with five seats; she took the last one and smiled a greeting to the other guests already seated. The event was at the point of opening speeches, and from the program which the usher had provided, she realized there would also be a lengthy lecture.

Stifling a weary sigh, Sifon wished she'd gotten here later. At least, she'd have missed the officious speeches and lectures. But then, she had to make a good impression on the commissioner if she was going to convince him of the viability of the hauling business.

It was a good thing, then, that the usher had seated her at a table close to the front; the commissioner nodded at her when he turned to peruse his guests. After that, boredom took over, and she fought to keep her eyes open; the stress of the day was catching up with her. Checking her wristwatch, she saw it was 9:12 p.m., and she vaguely wondered when and if she'd be able to speak with the commissioner.

***

Manny was ready to pull out his hair at the third speech and the imminence of a lengthy lecture before the award proper. He was only there because the awardee, the Commissioner for Infrastructure and Rural Development, was a serial guest at his various resorts. Besides, he'd personally invited him to the event, so there was no way he could avoid it, not when having friends like the commissioner was important.

He'd toyed with the idea of leaving and then dropping off a case of wine as an apology and congratulation wrapped in one. But all that flew from his brain when his gaze left his phone to study the guests in a bid to reduce his boredom, only to latch onto a familiar heart-shaped face.

His stomach flipped and warmed at the sight of her. She obviously hadn't seen him, and couldn't, not while her eyes looked half-mast as though struggling with sleep. And she wasn't wearing glasses; did she have her contacts on? Manny couldn't blame her, he was equally tired of the event, and it was quite unfortunate that he had another one he had to attend after this.

After being rude to her at his resort's dining room, he'd not stopped thinking about her and the ways he could apologize and get back in the good graces of Joshua, who, true to his word, hadn't called, answered when he called or replied to any of his messages.

Manny had considered speaking to Dora but reasoned that she might have the need to tell her friend about the drama playing out because of her. There was no need to give Sifon more edge than she already had on him, so, he'd ignored the need to call her, and was sort of glad when he couldn't find the card Joshua had dropped.

It was absolutely embarrassing that he'd been acting like a kid, wet behind the ears with his first female, but this was what he'd become — an old man panting after a girl who could be his daughter. Manny had scoffed at men who'd felt the need to consort with younger women, and mentally spat at their indecency.

But finding himself unconsciously having sensual imaginings about her naked body had caused him numerous sleepless nights. He was disgusted at himself.

This feeling wasn't right. He shouldn't be imagining how it would feel to grab her tender neck while he slid into her moistness, her innocent eyes dazed in passion while her breasts jiggled from his thrusts...

A sudden burst of applause broke off his dirty thoughts. He immediately looked to where she sat and saw that she had sat up and joined the applause. Manny did the same, his eyes not leaving her through the event.

His gaze stayed on her as she edged close to where the commissioner was taking photographs with other dignitaries and wondered if she was one of those women who loved taking selfies with big men to show off their connections.

But she never brought out her phone and never joined the people struggling to take photographs with the tired-looking awardee. Instead, Sifon kept checking her wristwatch and shifting her weight from one foot to the other.

Manny hung around, hiding in plain view as he monitored her movements. Unfortunately, he couldn't not admire her beautiful figure in a peach silk blouse, tucked into a dark blue below-the-knee-length pleated skirt. His gaze went to her feet and he unconsciously smiled when he saw that her heel, though high, was balanced as opposed to the pencil kind other ladies tottered about in; always sensible.

She no longer had braids, and her short hair was combed backward in a sleek do that shaped her small head, adding to her subtle beauty. Yet, men and women stared. The women stared as women do, probably admiring her outfit or being jealous, but the men were the ones that gave him concern. They stared as though they were carnivores about to pounce on a juicy piece of meat.

Manny had to curb the pressing need to go stand by her with his hand on her lower back to stake his claim. He shook his head to clear the barbaric thought; he convinced himself that he was only waiting to get the belated apology out of the way and, of course, restore his amiable relationship with Joshua. With Irene not in the picture, he was bored, and lonely, and needed someone to freely converse with.

Finally, the commissioner gave Sifon audience, and Manny watched her speak passionately, answering questions the man posed. He had an idea what their discussion must be about, but he wanted to hear it first-hand.

As though they heard his thought, the commissioner placed his hand on the small of her back and moved her towards the entrance. A growl rose in his throat but cut off when Sifon moved away from his touch, leaving a respectable space between them. "Good girl," he muttered, releasing a breath he hadn't realized he'd been holding and drawing close to where they stood.

The commissioner's eyes were shifty in their sockets, glancing at her chest often until she stopped talking, before he sighed gustily and looked up at the people hanging around waiting to see him. That was when he sighted Manny and grinned at him.

"Manny! I'm so glad you could make it." Manny swore under his breath as the commissioner extended his hand, beckoning him over, and his eyes finally met

Sifon's smile, which seemed a bit strained. These were the kind of men that made him hate his feelings for her.

"It was a wonderful event, congratulations again." Manny shook his hand and waited to be introduced to Sifon as etiquette dictated, but that never happened.

"So, my dear young girl," he turned to Sifon again, though his hand remained on Manny's forearm, obviously to hold him down while he dismissed the 'young girl'. "Your ideas are fantastic, but eh, I just wish you had come with your male partner. Because, looking at you and how beautifully feminine you are..." Here he chuckled, looking at Manny to share in his joke, but he just grimaced, hating what was unfolding. "...I am sceptical that the venture will flourish. But if you need my assistance in any other capacity, I'll be willing." He concluded his speech grinning and perusing Sifon's body.

How the hell was her facial expression still calm; how could she even be smiling while Manny was ready to tear off the arsehole commissioner's head? Then he recalled how he'd treated her at the resort, and guilt suffused his heart, almost choking him.

"Oh, okay. May I speak freely, Sir?" Her expression remained polite.

The commissioner threw open his arms, grinning and nodding. "Of course," he agreed.

How, in God's name, did the stupid man not see what was coming? Manny had only sat down with her once, for less than ten minutes. And in that time, despite his rudeness, he'd not seen the hard glint that presently shone in her eyes. Despite her polite tone, Manny didn't know how he knew, he just had a strong and sure feeling that nothing she'd say to the commissioner at this point would in any way be polite.

Sifon shifted close and further reduced the tone of her voice, looking the man in the eye. "I want to thank you, Sir, for the magnanimity of even agreeing to see me, despite it all having been a charade to add to your bogus personality."

"What?" The commissioner frowned, shifting his head back to look at Sifon. Manny thought that perhaps he hadn't heard right, since her demeanour remained polite, the smile never wavering. Sifon pulled him close with a strong tug of his sleeve. Manny recalled his mother doing that in his pre-teens when he'd overplayed at an event and she'd not wanted to scold him in the hearing of other guests.

"Yes, don't look confused, what you think you heard is what I said."

"Young lady, who do you think you're talking to? Manny, can you imagine this—"

"Cease your blathering!" The commissioner was shocked into silence for a second, and he bristled, but Sifon continued before he could rally his thoughts to speak. "If you make a fuss, I will give you a loud reply that I'm sure your wife wouldn't appreciate, and neither would your guests. So, just allow me to finish what I have to say."

"What arrant—? Manny..."

"Will Manny save you when I insinuate your offer to sleep with me...right here?"

Manny swallowed hard, feeling the pressing tension in their small circle while struggling with his pride for Sifon. "Err, Sir, let the young lady speak her mind and be done with it," he pleaded, even though he wanted to beat the man to a pulp. He wished for the past, his past; the commissioner wouldn't have survived the night with his teeth intact. So, if he couldn't express his anger, he would give Sifon the opportunity to.

The commissioner frowned at Manny and then grudgingly flicked his hand. "Speak."

"I've run my company for three years, and it has succeeded, unlike the many ventures you have failed at. Don't look so shocked, Commissioner; a good businessperson does his or her research before approaching an investor. And let me further bust your bubble: you were in our list of no probability. I am only here because you shocked us by agreeing to a meeting.

"And, alas, it was a good thing my partner decided to spend quality time with his fiancée rather than be here at this pretentious event with your pretentious award. Apparently, I gave you more credit than you deserved, unlike my partner."

"I will not listen to this—"

Sifon laughed loudly, turning the heads of guests waiting at the periphery of their circle. She focused on the man again. "That's how loud I can be."

The commissioner swallowed hard, shifting his weight with a petulant frown, reminding Manny of a scolded child forced to do what he didn't want to do.

"Next time, desist from giving false hope to start-up business owners in a bid to fan the flames of your bogus personality. I had a long, hard day at work and would have been resting instead of being here. You have taken hours of my time I'm never getting back because of your empty-headedness. Behave like the big man you claim to be. Nobody will beat you if you say no outright."

Sifon straightened, sighed, and smiled, as though relieved. "Good talk. I believe I'll go say hello to Mrs. Greg." She included Manny in her smile. "Good evening, gentlemen," she said and sashayed away.

It took seconds for what she had said to sink into the commissioner's mind, and then he started, tightening his hold on Manny. "That's my wife...Mrs. Greg...that's my wife she wants to...Manny, do something," he whispered.

"What do you want me to do?" Manny whispered back...except, stomp to Sifon and hug the breath out of her. She'd been phenomenal, and he wanted her. There was no need denying it anymore; he wanted her now more than ever.

Though he wanted to rush to her, he waited with the commissioner, who sounded like he was wheezing as Sifon picked her way through the crowd until she stood regally before Mrs. Greg.

"Jesus, what is she saying...what do you think she's saying? That girl is a witch."

Manny turned exasperated eyes to the man, then with an unobtrusive head shake, he looked away, swallowing the things he wished to say to the useless man. He saw his wife smile amiably at Sifon, who bent her knees in respectful greeting before walking out of the hall. He rushed his goodbyes to the worried commissioner and marched out, spying Sifon's retreating figure heading to the car park.

A wave of indecision slammed into him as he made to follow her, slowing his strides to mere tottering as he wondered whether to approach her or not, especially after the unpleasant episode with the commissioner. He needed to apologize, but was it the right time? He wanted her badly, but what was he offering; did he want her as a mistress?

With a muttered curse, he gave up trying to second-guess himself and half-jogged after her. Manny caught her unlocking her car, and she looked up and groaned when she saw him.

"I'm so sorry."

"For what?" She was exasperated.

"Well...err...for the time at the resort?"

"Are you asking me or apologizing?" Her exasperation doubled. "Besides, that was almost three weeks ago, and like I told Joshua, you had your reasons. Plus, it isn't wise to cajole anyone into business."

"That sort of defeats the whole purpose of being partners. All partners in a venture need to have the same conviction of success. This has been a driving policy for me."

"Right." She looked away, the floodlight that illuminated the parking lot glinting off her dangling earring. Her tone was grudgingly accepting, and Manny suspected she might be hiding a smile.

Manny drew close and inhaled sharply when a lazy breeze ruffled her hair, blowing her mouth-watering fragrance to him. Sifon turned to him again, her right elbow on the roof of her car, her mien calm and comported.

"I like...people, who own their mistakes and aren't fidgety in their apology. I appreciate people who don't beat about the bush." She said this raising both eyebrows at him. Manny felt she was giving him a subtle hint; it took him seconds to get.

He drew closer, his eyes looking into hers, when he saw them flicker with a smidgeon of what he'd been feeling...was she also attracted to him? His eyes dropped to the ticking pulse at the base of her neck. He caught her swallowing with some difficulty, and his gaze rose to hers again, this time in discernment. She liked him, but how did he go about expressing his feelings while corralling their emotions to a casual consort?

"I apologize for being rude to you by the pool that night. It was totally unnecessary."

"I agree." She cleared her throat, hiding another smile by ducking her head.

Manny bit his lower lip to curb his need to caress her soft brown cheek and smooth tendrils of her hair from her lovely face.

"I am terribly sorry for being an even greater arsehole in the morning."

"Hmm." She flung her head backwards, moaning as though he'd caressed her somewhere erotic. "I love your apology, and it's accepted." She smiled at him, a genuine smile. Manny knew this because her eyes were warm. Then she slid into her car and tried to drag the door closed, but he held on.

"Hey, you can't go like that," Manny panicked.

"Why not?" She didn't sound angry, just curious, but it didn't stop her from sliding her key into the ignition.

Because he was captivated with her and wanted more time to figure her out. But he said instead, "Because we have unfinished business. I want to know the investment opportunities in Joshfon Limited and their viability."

Sifon's hands dropped from the steering wheel to her lap, her head bent in consideration while staring at him. "Is this because of what happened in there?" She flicked her hand at the direction of the hall.

Manny wanted to avoid her piercing gaze. He felt like she might discern the actual reason he wanted her to stay. He shrugged, "Not exactly. I've wanted to call you for weeks now. I got your card from Joshua but, ah, I've wanted to call so many times, I've lost count." He chuckled and scratched his mat of a beard in embarrassment, mentally wondering why he'd confessed that.

Her eyes widened, and then she chuckled along with him. "That sounds like gist for another time. I really had a long day, and I'd want my wits about me when we discuss business."

"You flatter an old man."

"There's nothing old about you except your silver beard."

They locked gazes, and in the tension that ensued, Manny felt more was said in the silence than they'd ever actually spoken. He took a deep breath to calm his pounding heart and shut her car door. "I'll call you. For lunch, perhaps?" He straightened his white native jumper and cleared his throat when his voice came out a bit hoarse.

"I'd love that." She smiled and turned her ignition, but nothing happened.

CHAPTER SIX

A line from the movie Coming to America, where the prince and his friend attended a Black awareness event, popped into his mind — *There is a God...somewhere!*

Manny tightened his jaw to curb any show of excitement. He was torn between being giddy that he'd have more time with her and worried that her car had issues; what if he'd not been there, especially this late? Refusing to entertain that scenario, he concentrated on being glad that he got to play her hero.

"Okay, Sifon, enough. You've tried it a gazillion times, I don't think it's going to turn on tonight. Besides, you'll end up killing your battery, and that'll only compound the issue."

After pleading for over fifteen minutes, she finally heeded his prods and grudgingly climbed out of the car. Manny vaguely wondered why she was driving this beat up car when Joshua drove a beautiful SUV that he'd bought from his share of profits from the company. There was obviously a story there, and he planned to know it.

"A gazillion times?" She gave him a small smile and shook her head when he grinned.

Rather than ask for her car key, he drew close, his starched jumper touching her delicate blouse. His breath disturbed tendrils of hair on her temple as he reached for her right hand, caressing her wrist before gripping the key, lightly scraping her palm in the process and smiling when she gasped.

"Have you gotten everything from the car?" His question came out in a low growl. He was seconds from pulling her to him and kissing her succulent lips.

Sifon jerked and stepped back from him. "Err..." She licked her lips, seeming nervous. "Err...I think I have. Oh, wait, I have an overnight bag in the trunk." She hurried to the trunk and then turned to him when she realized she didn't have her key.

"Got it." Manny opened the trunk using the latch beside the driver's seat. "Why do you have an overnight bag?" He blurted what he'd been thinking without censor, worried that she might have been heading to her boyfriend's place; why else would a lady have an overnight bag in her car?"

Sifon glanced at him, her eyes narrowing at his tone. "The bag is a fixture in my car because we have to pull all-nighters at the office most times when we have a backlog of orders to receive and deliver."

"Shit," he muttered under his breath and proceeded to lock her car.

"Mm-hmm," Sifon smiled, seeming to know what he'd been thinking.

He cleared his throat. "I'll handle this. My auto-diagnostics guy will be here tomorrow to take care of it," he explained as he led her to his 2018 Infiniti QX80. Manny opened the passenger door and helped her inside before he rounded to the driver's side to turn the ignition and flick on the air conditioner.

It took him a couple of minutes to inform the Guest House management that his car had broken down at their lot and that his mechanic would be coming to tow it in the morning. Manny dropped his card and a tip for the receptionist to call him before handing over the key to the mechanic, and then hurried back to his car.

"So, where do you live?"

Sifon flinched and emitted a heavy sigh. "Ifa, down Oron road."

"What the f—" He held himself from uttering the curse word; he knew where it was. "Why so far from town?"

"Because my house is there?" she teased.

"You know what I mean," he smiled, reversing in the almost empty parking lot.

"My mom built her house there. It's awesome that I don't have to pay rent in these difficult times."

Manny nodded. "I hear real estate in Uyo is a goldmine."

She shrugged, "I guess." The small movement brought another waft of her perfume and Manny inhaled with relish, but then he recalled that he still had one party to attend before he called it a night.

"Fuck!"

"You know, for an oldie, you curse a lot," she chuckled.

"I'm sorry, I just…"

"No need to apologize…it's sexy."

His heart stuttered and then continued beating, only faster. "Err…umm… There's this party at the Estate that I have to attend. It's the birthday of a close friend; I have his gift with me. We'll just spend ten, twenty minutes, tops, and then I'll take you straight home. Please?" he added, glancing at her.

Sifon smiled. "There's no need to plead. I know the stress I'd have suffered to get home at this time; Opay would have been dicey, and Taxify would require a limb to get me home. So, you're doing me a great favour. You're my knight in white kaftan."

Manny couldn't recall laughing that freely in a while…and with a woman. When Irene hadn't been obsessed with marriage, she'd been more concerned with appearances than fun conversations. He dabbed a tear from the corner of his eye as he manoeuvred the SUV into a street, and then struggled to avoid a pothole when her fingers delicately swiped his upper cheek, presumably wiping off the residue of tears from his humour.

His gasp was louder than the whispery radio in the vehicle. "Goddamnit! Your touch should come with a warning." His tone came off gruffer than intended, and he only realized it when Sifon jerked her hand away and seemed to lean towards the door, creating space between them.

Struggling with the lightning effect of her touch, his limbs shook as he pressed the accelerator, shoving the car forward on the dark, empty road. Just when he sighed, trying to relieve the regret in his chest and apologize for snapping at her, his phone buzzed in the console between them, the screen lighting up with the name of his friend's personal assistant.

"I'm close to the house," he answered with no pleasantries. And real anger unfurled in the pit of his stomach when the young man told him the birthday had been shifted from the celebrant's home to Le Meridien - Ibom Hotel and Golf Resort, the Akwa Ibom five-star hotel.

"This is the sort of information you give before time," he snapped, and the guy quickly explained that he'd sent an SMS earlier and the call was just follow-up.

He ended the call with a furrowed brow. "We have to get to Le Meridien."

***

Manny's comment came out in a growl, and Sifon wondered if it was still as a by-product of her touch.

She didn't understand him. After his apology, he'd become playful, and she'd loved every moment of their flirting...or wasn't he flirting with her, had she misread him?

Shame warmed her face at the thought. She'd called him sexy, for God's sake, no wonder he hadn't commented when she'd said it, he was probably wondering about her sanity. And she'd thought his stammer after the sexy comment had been cute. What had she been thinking? How had she allowed her fantasies about him to slip into reality?

While he'd been on the phone, she'd tried to calm her breathing by silently sucking in the cool AC air to slow her racing heart and blow away her embarrassment. Her left hand was folded on her lap, burning from the feel of his tender skin. Warmth had unfurled in her belly at the contact. She wanted to touch him again.

Sifon shook her head to erase the untoward wish; do not embarrass yourself again, she silently admonished herself. She missed their earlier camaraderie in the face of the tomb silence that engulfed them as they drove to the prestigious resort. Well, it wasn't exactly tomb silent because the radio twittered some sounds, and Manny kept sighing heavily, like he was garnering the courage to say something. Perhaps an apology? Sifon mentally shook her head; there was no need to let the fantasies in again.

Whoever was celebrating a birthday at the five-star hotel must be rich and famous. Sifon vaguely wondered if she could interest the person in an investment opportunity. She wasn't sure of Manny and Joshua had expressed his dislike for Udeko, so it was pertinent to resume sourcing for other possible investors.

With the roads almost free of vehicular activity at a few minutes past 11 p.m., they arrived at the hotel in thirteen minutes. If the loud music wasn't an indication that there was a celebration, the line-up of cars, which made parking difficult, was a glaring sign. Manny was lucky to find a spot close to the entrance when someone pulled out.

Manny's heavy sighs continued as they neared the entrance and the automatic doors opened, but Sifon refused to give meaning to them; he was old, after all, maybe he had a heart condition.

Sifon flinched at the terrible thought, her heart squeezing painfully at the notion that he was ill. She glanced sideways at him, appreciating his height. Not many people his age were as tall as him, or as fit. He was trim; she recalled how his t-shirt had draped over his muscled frame at the pool party, and now his white jumper stretched across his broad chest. He obviously worked out. He didn't sound breathless as he walked beside her, yet, she still couldn't find meaning to his heavy sighs.

The thump of the music engulfed her thoughts as she stared at the magnificent party before her. The event was happening right in the centre of the hotel, the first thing one saw when they walked through the doors. Guests sat on decorated seats and tables around the raised, circular platform which had gushing beatific fountains in the centre and along the edge. On the wooden circular platform, arranged like a sitting room with leather chairs, low coffee tables, and potted plants, Sifon assumed the celebrant sat with his VVIP guests.

People close to the entrance were already greeting Manny. Sifon walked quietly beside him. She plucked a glass of champagne from a passing waiter and gulped the whole thing. Manny watched her as she stopped another waiter, returned the empty glass and gulped down another one, blocking the black and white-dressed server from moving with her hand on his arm.

"Sifon?" She almost choked as she gulped the third glass, hoping it was fortifying enough for the amount of time she'd have to spend here with the owner of the voice behind her.

"Hmm," she answered, swallowing the last of the drink, returning the flute and letting the server finally pass. She turned to him with widened eyes, her gaze taking in his trimmed salt and pepper beard. She wanted to bury her fingers in the short bristles, scattering and smoothing them along his strong jaws all day and night, especially at night.

Manny frowned at her, seeming puzzled by something, Sifon didn't know what. She only knew that she was suddenly pressed, and she had to meander to the convenience on the other side of the hall; having been here before, she knew where it was. The distance seemed too far, and her bladder became quite heavy, as though she'd just guzzled a tank of water instead of a mere three flutes of champagne.

"I have to go to the ladies'," she said, after he'd not said anything, having to shout to be heard over the music because there was no way she was leaning close to speak into his ear; she would be inundated with his sexy scent and she would not be held responsible for nibbling on his ear. She shifted to the side and walked round him to begin her journey to the convenience.

Sifon gasped at the shock that went through her entire body when his hand grabbed her wrist, holding her in place. At that moment, even her bladder ceased to be heavy, the pressing need to urinate vanished. She turned, her gaze going straight to where they were joined. Manny must have recalled his earlier snapped words of touches coming with warnings, because he snatched his hand off when he followed her gaze.

That wasn't what her look meant; she didn't want his hand off her, she wanted more.

"I'm sorry."

Sifon widened her eyes questioningly at him, and he shifted his weight from one foot to the other, his eyes flitting from her face to the party and back.

He coughed into his hand and drew close. "For sounding rude in the car. I wasn't angry or anything, I was just shocked, taken unawares and—"

"Apology accepted," she interrupted sharply, stepping back. "I really have to pee." Sifon swivelled and marched round the periphery of the party, hurrying away from Manny's intoxicating scent and the near accident of licking his neck as he spoke into her ear.

***

Your touch should come with a warning — goddamnit, why had he said that? With the way he was muddling along, he would be apologizing to her all the time.

Manny watched her hurry away, worried that he'd messed up his slim chances with her. But, damn it, she couldn't blame him for his reaction. She'd just called him sexy, made him laugh, and then touched him unexpectedly, not even giving him a chance to brace for the impact. The effect had been as though she'd brushed his half-aroused dick in the midst of people; it was both amazing and appalling.

He sighed, shoved his left hand into his pocket and scratched his beard with his right, wondering what he could do to return them to that point of light banter and laughter.

"She doesn't seem so taken with you, Manny."

The temporary lull in music carried the smug tone to Manny's ears, and his mind recognized the unmistakable owner of the voice. Another heavy sigh thundered from his mouth before he turned.

"It's been a while, Koko," Manny greeted pleasantly, looking at the average height man, a friend turned brother and then enemy, whose face twisted into disdain, erasing all earlier smugness.

"You lost the right to call me that when you left!"

Manny nodded at his fierce whisper, looking around and nodding when nobody seemed interested in them. He turned to him again. "I'm sorry, Mr. Udeko." The sarcasm was obvious.

"Fuck you, Manny. Despite all your sanctimonious exploits, you are, at the end of the day, still human and muddy like the rest of us. You can't escape it."

"I never said I wasn't human, Udeko."

"But you wouldn't let us rest with your gospel against old men and young maidens," Udeko's smugness returned.

Here lay the issue with Sifon. Anybody who knew him was aware that he never had sexual dealings with women way younger than him. "She could be my staff."

"But she isn't," Udeko scoffed.

Manny shook his head, smiling to hide his building fury. He didn't want to discuss Sifon with this despicable man from his past. "You wouldn't know that."

"Oh, but I do, Manny. You see, she's been marked to finally clean my money."

* * *

After relieving herself and cleaning up, Sifon was just about to press the steel flusher on the wall when two chattering ladies walked into the convenience, each choosing a stall to handle their business while still conversing.

One had just asked the other who the sexy, white-bearded man was, and her hand stilled, heart thumping, unconsciously waiting for the reply.

"Oh, that's the owner of Manny Resorts, everybody calls him Manny. I hear he changes women like underwear."

Sifon gasped, covering her mouth to keep from coughing, her heart squeezing painfully at the thought of Manny with so many women.

"Are you sure? Because I overheard Francis telling my husband that he's not married and doesn't frolic with younger women, just people closer to his age. He can't be changing women like underwear when available women close to his age are next to zero in this Uyo."

The gossip, as Sifon had immediately dubbed her, scoffed, "Do you know the number of married women that cheat in this town?"

"I know. But, if he has the discipline to stay away from younger women, a trending exploit among men his age, and he isn't even married, why then would he mess with a married woman?"

"Madam Lawyer, me, I'm just giving you gist," she scoffed again in humour, both toilets flushing almost at once. Sifon remained in her stall, barely breathing.

The other woman laughed as they stepped out and proceeded to the wall of sinks to wash their hands. "I know it's just gist. I was admiring his physique. He could have passed for a younger man if not for his white beard. I wish our husbands would put in some effort to, at least, reduce their stomach sizes."

Laughing mockingly, the gossip replied, "Fufu and Afang will not allow."

"And pounded yam with Afia-efere ebot, where the pieces of goat meat are like hulks in the soup."

Both women laughed, heading to the door. "So true, the other day, my husband almost..."

The sound of music increased as they opened the door, drowning out their words. Sifon let out her breath in a whoosh, flushing the toilet with the same momentum. Now, she had no idea what to believe about Manny.

Sifon shook her head as she rinsed soap suds from her hands while eyeing her shiny neck-length black hair. Having just taken down her braids and washed it, she'd had to use her hand dryer and hair tongs to straighten the strands and had put on her statement earrings to look presentable for the commissioner's event.

Why the hell was she even thinking of her hair instead of Manny's hesitation when it came to her? She wasn't that young; at thirty in the next couple of months, she wasn't so young for him.

Who even cared about age these days? Manny cares, her nosy mind replied. Sifon's fingers scrunched from being under the tap too long. With a scoff at herself and her almost uncontrollable need for Manny, she wiped her hands, took a deep breath and joined the roaring party.

There were older men everywhere, wealthy older men, most of them married, and she felt nothing for them, not even the generic admiration she usually had for sensible older people. All her emotions had pooled for just one man, who restrained from their clear chemistry because she was younger.

Shaking her head, she picked her way to the spot she'd left him, but slowed when he wasn't there or anywhere near. He would never abandon her here, she thought while scanning the crowd.

Sifon pulled out her phone while worrying if her sharp answer to his apologetic explanation had made him leave. Hadn't he heard she'd been going to the ladies'; did he think she'd been leaving?

The brilliance from her phone shone in her eyes before she recalled she didn't have Manny's number. She blinked and looked up; she was uncomfortable wearing her contacts for hours, which is why she only wore them for events. She would have been home if her car hadn't broken down, having removed them by now and probably struggling to sleep with Manny always on her mind.

She elected to call Joshua and get Manny's number, deciding she wouldn't be angry that he'd left; she would plead for him to come get her and, at least, drop her in town where she could easily get a Taxify home, no matter how expensive. It was a case of misunderstanding.

Getting a taxi at the hotel this late would be next to impossible. Or maybe she could get a ride from one of the guests leaving? The thought stalled her fingers from clicking the dial button, which was when a shadow darkened where she stood.

Sifon felt someone was passing, so she stepped aside, barely registering the person. But when the shadow followed, she looked up with an irked expression and found an older woman who looked like she was about to scratch someone's eyes out. It couldn't be her; she'd just been standing here worrying about how she'd get home.

The woman was pretty in her maturity. It was immediately obvious that she took care of herself and was careful about her appearance, even though the jewellery was too much. She looked like someone Manny would go for.

And the thought had barely registered in her mind when the woman spoke.

"So like Manny to abandon his whore when he's done using her."

Sifon's eyes widened and her mouth popped open — what?

"Oh, don't take it personal, he does that with a lot of other people," she flicked her wrist with a throaty laugh.

Despite her muddled thoughts, Sifon vaguely wondered if Manny knew that he had some haters among his counterparts. She took a deep breath. Having recovered from the initial shock of the woman's attack, she prepared to politely insult her when the woman's eyes shifted from her to someone over her shoulder.

Before long, Manny's unique scent engulfed her with a warmth that seemed like a hug. It took a second for Sifon to realize that Manny, indeed, had put his arm around her waist, pulled her flush to his body, and was kissing the side of her head.

Her knees did the sensible thing and weakened from the onslaught of warm emotions his act rained on her, but as the hero he was, his strong arm held her up. She sighed with relief and looked up to his smiling face, his eyes warm for her.

"I thought you'd left," she whispered.

His eyes flickered for a moment, like maybe he was hurt she'd not had a level of faith in him. He shook his head with a small smile, "And leave you here with all these animals?"

"I'd wondered that about my sexy hero in white kaftan." Sifon gave him a coy through-the-lashes gaze she hoped was seductive.

Manny broke into a deep chuckle, pulling her closer even though she was already plastered to his side. "I'm sorry you wondered that. I'd rushed outside to get the gift for Francis' PA."

Sifon nodded while recalling the women in the convenience had mentioned a Francis, obviously the celebrant. She turned to the momentarily shocked woman who had been following their little exchange and couldn't resist looking smug.

She felt Manny take a deep breath. "Irene," he greeted, and Sifon stiffened, realizing he knew her. But before envy could crawl from her abdomen to her throat, Manny extended his hand from her hip to her belly, tenderly caressing the side. Of course, all other emotions vanished for swooning.

"Is this who you replaced me with, just because I refused to pick your calls for a couple of weeks?" The older woman was bringing on the malice.

Sifon scanned the party and was happy no one paid them any mind; the music and conversations created a cocoon for this confrontation.

"Irene, please, get your facts right. You stormed out of my house with your things approximately five months ago, and I stopped calling four months plus ago when I got the message that it was obviously over between us."

"So, you've decided to try out young girls after preaching against it for years," she sneered, and Sifon felt him stiffen, his fingers pressing into her soft stomach.

Unconsciously, Sifon reached up and covered his hand on her stomach, silently comforting his agitation. It must have worked, because his breath ruffled her hair, and she felt him relax.

"Believe whatever helps you sleep at night, Irene." He straightened, looking down at Sifon. "Let's go say hi to Francis, and then home?"

Sifon smiled at him, making sure it expressed adoration. "Sure," she purred, grinning when the older woman huffed and stomped to the entrance.

CHAPTER SEVEN

"You have a lovely home."

Grunt.

That was the only reply she'd gotten since she'd agreed to spend the night at his place so he could drop her off by daybreak, seeing as it was too late and rather dangerous to be heading to the semi-rural community where her house was located.

Hadn't he meant it when he'd offered, or had he just been being polite?

"I'll show you to the guest room," he growled, preceding her into a corridor that presumably led to the room.

Oh, he speaks, was her acerbic thought, rolling her eyes as she followed him. Manny was really confusing, and she was tired of the hot and cold vibes he'd been giving. This was the kind of thing that made her stay away from relationships. Men could be such kids, she sighed heavily.

Manny turned with an expression akin to concern. "Are you okay?"

Really? Sifon gave him an eyebrow lift, then shook her head when he just frowned, obviously not understanding. "I'm really tired." It wasn't a lie, it was 1:17 a.m., after all.

His mouth twitched as though he wanted to say something, but then he frowned and continued down the corridor. He opened a door, walked in, and flicked on the light.

Sifon sighed when she saw the fluffy bed. She briskly walked with her arms stretched before her and fell face down on the amazing bed, groaning in relief.

A peek from the side of her eye showed her that Manny had strode beyond the bed to switch on the AC.

She twisted and lay on her back with her sandaled feet scuffing the luxurious fur that passed as a carpet. She sucked in a deep breath and sighed in appreciation. The room smelled like him, and it was making her feel things she shouldn't be feeling.

To erase the sensual feeling stealing through her veins, she decided to focus on the pain in her feet. "God, my feet are killing me," she groaned.

The problem was, Sifon hadn't expected Manny to quietly go on one knee by the bed, unbuckle her sandals and, with utmost care, lift her feet to his bent knee and massage them with soft but firm strokes.

There was no way she could have curbed the appreciative moan that erupted from her throat, even if she'd tried. Shame suffused her body, but on the tail of that, the sensual feeling she'd been trying to ignore bubbled into a burn. It was as though embarrassment and eroticism were bordered by a thin line.

Sifon bit her lower lip, forbidden pictures dancing behind her closed eyes, pictures that would shock Manny if he knew. His touch on her feet caused a direct reaction to her pussy. Her lady parts went wet, as though her arches were buttons to open a flood of sexual excitement between her thighs.

Unconsciously, she pressed her knees together, twisting slightly to manage the unrelenting ache that thoughts of Manny usually caused. This was the reason she'd not been having restful nights. This ache was the reason she shamelessly needed relief, even in her dreams, but it never came.

The reality, on the other hand, was more intense than what her mind could have conjured. If she was ready to fling her legs wide for him from just an innocent foot massage, what would happen when those hands became seductive?

"Fuck!" Manny dropped her legs and surged to his feet so abruptly, his knee banged the wood of the bed.

Sifon flinched. "Oh! Sorry," she commiserated, raising herself on her elbow, her breath coming in pants, for once again, she was unfulfilled because of this man.

Manny turned from her, as though the sight of her was an abomination. "Good night," he grumbled, his long strides allowing him to reach the still open door of the room before she could blink.

"Wait!"

He refused to turn, and it irked Sifon because it could also mean that the sight of her disgusted him. She struggled to her feet, marched to where he stood, grabbed his muscular arm and pulled.

It didn't happen as she'd envisioned it, his bulk being too heavy for her one-handed manoeuvre. With a sigh that got his broad shoulders drooping, he turned to face her with an exasperated expression.

Sifon didn't like that; it made her feel like a petulant kid, which was not how she wanted to feel with him. With need and anger struggling for supremacy in her chest, she went on tiptoe while her right hand flew to his neck, rounded it and pulled.

She mentally smiled when she saw the shock on his face just before she swallowed his lips in a kiss she'd wanted since that first night by the pool.

Manny groaned into her mouth, and she responded with a moan of her own, enjoying his smoky taste and the scratch of his beard on her chin. She drew close, rounding both arms on his neck and plastering her body on the length of his.

It was then she found why he must have dropped her legs as though they burned him; Manny had been as affected as she'd been. The evidence lay stiff against her belly, jerking as their tongues tangled, their noses brushing as their heads moved from side to side, lost in the euphoria of their kiss.

The problem was he was always running away, apparently driven by the age factor.

This kiss was to show him that she found him attractive and that she wanted to go all the way with him; his age didn't bother her. The kiss was also to punish him in retaliation for the late nights she'd suffered on his behalf; it didn't matter if he knew this or not.

Sucking a deep breath through her nose, she deepened the kiss, spearing her tongue into his mouth. She licked the roof of his mouth and he staggered. Sifon imagined the effect had weakened his knees, and she didn't mind that the movement slammed her back against the opened door. In fact, it fuelled the passion, almost making her forget that this was a punishment.

Their rough breaths filled the quiet of the room, the wet slurps of their lips driving Sifon so wild, her right hand left Manny's neck and plunged in between their bodies to his hardness poking her abdomen. She gasped, her eyes widening as she felt the length and strength of his dick.

Sweet mother grace! She wanted it in her right that moment, the weight and girth of it emphasizing the emptiness that had bludgeoned her since meeting him and not having him. She wanted that pronounced weight, girth, and length of him to fill her, she wanted his presence in her life, she wanted...

Sifon was close to offering herself right there, but she deepened the kiss, moaned, and bit his lower lip, before she wrenched herself from his embrace and pushed him away.

It so happened that the push propelled him just beyond the doorway. Sifon wasted no time in stepping back and slamming the door in his face, turning the lock for good measure. Her only regret was not seeing his reaction after the door slam.

****

Manny hadn't slept a wink.

How could he, with an erection that felt like a collection of all his other erections congregating to make one giant one that refused to go down, even after fucking his hand twice in the last thirty-five minutes?

Sighing for the umpteenth time, Manny reached down and grabbed his stiff cock, the length of it hot against his palm. It was both painful and amazing that he could stay aroused this long. And he knew it was because of her taste in his mouth, the memory of her softness against him, the whiff of her fragrance on his kaftan which he'd left lying by his pillow, unwilling to depart from it.

He hadn't been a very sexual person, even in his younger days as a smuggler with Joshua's father. He'd been okay with scratching an itch and walking away, never bothering with relationship hang-ups. But then he'd met his wife, Bukky, and he'd fallen over himself to marry her just so no other man would look at her, let alone talk of having her.

But even though he'd been possessive of Bukky and had never cheated on her, Manny had never felt this pressing amorousness he felt for Sifon. And even though she'd been his wife, and he'd been devoted to her — almost falling out with Etuk for impregnating Joshua's mother without marrying her, because he felt strongly about such things — Bukky had still cheated on him.

The cheating hadn't just been emotional, it'd been physical, and financial, as well, and it had led to her death. Later on, Irene had been convenient and he'd appreciated their arrangement, but she'd wanted more.

Manny shook his head to discard the gloomy thought. His late wife was the reason he would never traipse the aisle or trust a woman again. Which was why this thing with Sifon bothered him; it wasn't just her tender age — it was the title he would give her if he gave in to his desires.

Would she be his mistress? If she agreed, which he doubted, how long would it last? Would it be until she found a boyfriend her age? His heart squeezed at the notion. Therein lay the issue; even calling her his mistress in his thoughts made him cringe, and imagining her in another man's arms made him want to kill.

Then there was the comment Udeko had made. He could not trust a woman who had ties with Udeko. He was the man Bukky had cheated on him with. Manny should have been the one snapping angrily at the party, but their smuggling crew had always known Udeko to be a sanctimonious arsehole, who'd always get more incensed than expected, even when he was wrong.

Manny knew it was his defence mechanism for not being so smart and always being jealous, falling back on being devious to win. He'd known Udeko had wanted Bukky. What he'd not known was that she'd wanted him back.

Sighing heavily, he turned, pressing his nose to his kaftan, his half-hard dick jerking and hardening when he inhaled Sifon's scent. He wanted her, but as what? And he needed to know what deal she had with Udeko; was Joshua aware of it? He needed to be careful with her, and he needed to talk with Joshua.

He rolled again to his back, turned, and checked the clock on the bedside table. 4:15 a.m. There was no point trying to sleep. He'd do his exercises, take a bath and... His mind flashed a picture of going to Sifon's room and re-enacting that kiss, but he shook his head.

It had been a fluke; maybe she'd been drunk. Manny scoffed at the blatant lie. He'd wait for her to wake up, and then he'd take her home. He needed more time to think and make a decision.

CHAPTER EIGHT

Sifon hadn't slept at all.

It was a combination of many things. First off, the air in the room had the scent of him, and the AC only emphasized that fact. His fragrance kept her mind active with flashes of what had transpired by the door, and what could have transpired if Manny was one to give in. She rolled her eyes at the ceiling, then squinted when it hurt; she'd worn her contacts too long.

After she'd slammed the door in his face, she'd quickly discarded her clothes, dropped on the bed spread-eagled, shut her eyes to recall the feel and texture of him, his mouth, his taste, his hand hesitantly caressing her, and reached for her drenched cunt.

She'd stifled her moans when her fingers had gathered wetness from her cove and rubbed on her clitoris, the pleasure causing her hips to jerk from the bed as she gasped and imagined Manny's stubby fingers plunging into her. She'd come on a sharp sigh, but it'd not been enough at all. In fact, it had heightened her need for him to a point of frustration.

At 3:10 a.m., she'd been tempted to leave her room and search for his to force the issue. She'd never wanted a man this much. It wasn't a lie that she'd always told Dora that she preferred old guys; it'd been mainly because men of her generation just seemed clueless as to how to handle a smart, independent woman who knew what she wanted.

She'd shied away from relationships because she wasn't a patient person. Additionally, if it wasn't what she wanted, then she saw no reason for getting it. This policy had driven her aunt to distraction; the woman just wanted her to have a man, it didn't matter if she liked him or not.

Sifon liked and wanted Manny to a point of obsession. But it irked and confused her why he didn't want her. No, he wanted her, that much was obvious, but he was refusing to get her. She didn't understand; was he secretly married? She'd seen his ring, but with the way he'd spoken to Irene at the party, he wasn't. Sifon suspected he wore the ring to repel female attention.

Blowing out a sigh of frustration, she shoved from the bed and stood. The time on her phone read 3:57 a.m., a weird time, but she was hungry, and she hoped Manny had something to eat in his kitchen, even just a biscuit. When they'd returned earlier, she'd been too tired to consider food, but after that hot kiss, and the fact that she'd ingested lots of alcohol without food, she had to eat now or go delirious. Sifon considered her nightwear in the mirror, and as she lifted her arm, turning to check the length of the dress, she cringed when she smelled her armpit.

She recalled that she'd not taken a bath after the long night she'd had. With an exasperated sigh, she did just that. The time was 4:10 a.m. when she was ready to go find the kitchen; she was sure Manny would not be awake at this time. She hoped he lived alone, though he hadn't insinuated otherwise.

***

By 4:44 a.m., Manny marched out of his room as his own thoughts were suffocating him. He rubbed his chest as he walked down the corridor, pausing at the guest room and wondering if Sifon was asleep. Then he started wondering what she wore to bed. Was she naked?

With a disgusted sigh at himself, he shook his head and walked past the room, intending to wait in the sitting room for whenever she woke, so he could take her home and forget that the kiss had ever happened.

He was sure that by the time she woke, he'd have gotten himself together. He needed to cease this rubbish. Already, two of his counterparts had reminded him that he didn't do this sort of thing, he didn't consort with young...

Breath left him as he stepped into the sitting room, his eyes magnetically going to the light spilling from the kitchen, or specifically, the figure illuminated through the translucent shirt she wore.

His mouth felt like a desert. He couldn't take his eyes off Sifon, who stood at the counter in front of the lit bulb by the fridge, the only light she'd turned on. Manny could see everything — perhaps, not as clearly as the real deal, but close — and it didn't help him one bit.

He swallowed hard and had just decided to tiptoe out of there before she turned and found the tent in his joggers.

"Hey, good morning. Did I wake you? I'm sorry if I did. I was so hungry, I'm not sure I was as stealthy as I thought."

Why the hell did she sound so chirpy when it wasn't even five a.m.?

"Care for some? I toasted more bread than I could consume with the hope that you could have some when you wake. I'm sorry for taking the liberty, I was just really hungry."

She said all this still munching on the toasted sandwich in her hand; she didn't look sorry at all. And the aroma of whatever filling she'd used for the bread while she toasted it had sneaked to where he stood, making him recall he'd not eaten for hours.

Sifon kept chatting about all the liberties she'd taken in his kitchen, one that remained spotless because he never used it. She dusted crumbs from her hand before she moved to the cupboard beside the fridge where he kept his plates, which in turn provided another view of her wide hips and thick thighs.

Manny groaned and marched to the dining area while her back was still turned, his hands under his t-shirt to pull it over the monstrous bulge in his pants. He sat down with a huff and sighed as though he'd just escaped major catastrophe.

He was still trying to suck in breath to calm his traitorous body when she appeared beside him and placed a plate of sandwich triangles on the dining table. The aroma of the food was present, but he was inundated with her scent as she stood so close, her naked thigh touched his.

"Tea? I saw a pack of green tea on the fridge."

Shaking his head, he blew out a breath and squinted up at her freshly scrubbed-looking face with absolutely no make-up; it was another kind of beauty that took his breath away and caused him anguish.

"Why are you doing this?" he croaked and watched as her eyebrow lifted haughtily, then she turned swiftly to the kitchen.

"Juice it is," he heard her murmur.

She returned with a tray carrying her plate of sandwiches, two mugs, and a carton of mixed fruit juice. Humming under her breath, she placed the mugs and served the juice before taking the first seat on the right, close to the head of the table where he sat.

"Bon appétit," she sing-sang, biting into a sandwich triangle.

Manny left out another exasperated breath, folding his arms on his chest with a frown directed at her. "I asked you a question, Sifon?"

***

His authoritative tone did the opposite of what Manny had probably been aiming for; it turned her on. She bit her lower lip and pressed her thighs together.

Clearing her throat mildly, Sifon looked into his eyes. "What question?"

He groaned again and looked away then back with a more ferocious frown. "Just look at the way you're dressed," he pointed out piously.

"That's an honest mistake, Manny. I thought I'd be done and gone by the time you woke. Besides, if you don't feel anything for me, this shouldn't affect you."

Manny shook his head, looking up in exasperation. "Why me?"

"Because my body reacted to yours on sight."

He seemed shocked at her honesty, but in seconds, he covered it with a smirk. "Okay, so, it's just chemicals."

"Chemicals? You make it sound like it's gas, and in the event of my next big fart, my feelings will float into the atmosphere as though they never existed."

She watched his jaw harden after he'd scoffed an unwilling laugh. "So, what is it; infatuation, school girl crush... an old man fetish?"

Sifon clapped her palm to her mouth to hold back the juice that would have sprayed at her shocked laugh. "What?" She giggled with a frown at him, shoving a piece of sandwich into her mouth.

"Maybe you have daddy issues," Manny flung with a sigh, but the casualness of his comment didn't stop him from noticing she'd paused munching. He sat up immediately, his frown so thunderous it looked like he was about to kill somebody.

Could this snare him? Could it help him understand?

Sifon lightly cleared her throat as she swallowed her food, took a sip of juice, leaned on the high-backed chair and shrugged. "Perhaps. I did have a very handsome stepfather."

His growl vibrated the table. "Don't joke with something like this. Did he abuse you? Did your mom know? Is he alive?"

"Perhaps I abused him."

"Sifon, my God, is that what he forced you to say?"

A smile curved her mouth as she breathed through the pounding of her heart. She might have wanted to get him by any means, but this really was something that might have been a root cause of her wishing for an older man in a romantic relationship.

"No, I know I abused him."

Manny looked close to bursting an artery. "What the fuck? How?"

"Well—" She cleared her throat and licked her suddenly dry lips. "You'll be the third person aware of this event. The other two are myself and stepfather."

His jaw was so hard, Sifon feared for his teeth. But in order to be able to let out her dark secret, she had to not look at him, so she lowered her eyes.

"My dad died when I could barely recall his face, but my memories, happy memories, always had Uncle Joe in them. He was a fixture in my childhood, but then puberty happened."

"Jesus fucking Christ," he ground out, breathing through his mouth.

Sifon swallowed and lowered her eyes again. "Puberty meant I started having urges, and I understood the concept of romantic relationships, which my mother had with Joe. Apparently, Joe had been asking her to marry him for years. She finally agreed when I turned twelve."

"The problem here was, at this point, I had a schoolgirl crush, an unbreakable infatuation on Joe."

"So, he took advantage of it, right?"

"Nope, absolutely not." She shook her head, but then stared unseeingly at the painted portrait hanging in the sitting room. "Joe loved my mother too much to do such a thing. He was dedicated to her. Everyone, even I, could see he had eyes for her alone, and she'd made his dream come true by agreeing to marry him."

Manny grunted. It was a very angry and impatient sound.

"The problem was, I wanted exactly what my mother had; the fairy tale kind of love and romance that I saw in movies. They were really perfect together, and mother once shared with my aunt that Joe made her heart skip and pound and melt all at once."

"Life is too harsh for such delicate ideals to survive," Manny scoffed.

His words broke her heart. Sifon was tempted to let go and walk away. If she got Manny after this hot pursuit, it would only be to shatter her in the long run. His words spoke of someone who would never love, and that was exactly what she needed. The kind of love that would engulf her in warmth even at work, the kind that had her giddy and made her want to twirl. She was already halfway there with Manny, and it scared her that he didn't even believe in such emotion, talk more of feeling it.

With a deep breath, she countered, "Oh, but they do!"

He folded his arms again over his chest. "Does this story have a point?" he sneered.

Sifon swallowed to try and ease the pressure in her throat. "Yes, it does," she sighed. "I started looking for Joe in all my relationships, but never found him. Then, after ten years of marriage, my mother died and shattered all of us, except Joe ended up in even tinier pieces than I or my aunt."

Manny had sat up again, his arms loosening from his wide chest with an expression of commiseration. "I didn't know your mother was late."

"Well, now you know," she chuckled, trying to lighten the mood. "After the burial, Joe fell into a hole so deep and dark, he was barely lucid on some days. He started drinking. His friends couldn't help him, my aunt's prayers didn't seem to have any effect. I was left listening to his sobs every night, calling on my mother."

Sifon bit her lower lip as she recalled the weight of sorrow that had clouded their once happy home. "So, as a young adult full of ingenious ideas and a crush that hadn't disappeared..."

"Oh my God," Manny groaned, covering his face.

"I decided I could kill two birds with one stone. I could express my feelings while helping Joe."

"That's just—"

"So," she snapped, not wanting him to complete the derogatory-sounding sentence, "at the time, I was 22, and even though I wasn't as plump as my mom had been, I hoped I'd be enough for Joe, so, I went to his room."

"I don't want to hear this."

But Manny didn't get up, so she continued as though he'd not spoken. "Perhaps, his sobbing masked the sound of the opening door, or he might have been too drunk to notice or care. I really don't know which. I was just happy he hadn't chastised me for being there."

Manny's head dropped to his chest with a heavy sigh that ruffled his soft t-shirt.

"I joined him on the bed. Even though I wanted to seduce him, deep down, I also wanted to comfort him, so I called him my mother's pet name for him and to my happy shock, his arm rounded my waist and pulled me into his naked body. It was a dream come true of millions of fantasies. I pushed my luck and kissed him on the mouth despite his alcohol breath," her voice lowered while she recalled the night.

"He took over the kiss, moaning my mother's name, which I didn't mind at all, not while I was having a revelation. I was experiencing exactly what I'd been searching for in all my relationships."

"His eyes were closed while he kissed me, moaning against my lips. I revelled in the heat of his muscular body," Sifon sighed and closed her eyes to better recall. Manny's roar broke the reverie. Her eyes flew open to witness his chair tumbling behind him as he stood and stalked from the dining area to his room.

Sifon panted, realizing how deep she'd been in the memory. She licked her dried lips, her hand sliding down in between her thighs to find she was soaked. Of course, she was. After all, for the first time since the experience, that memory didn't have Joe's face, it had Manny's.

CHAPTER NINE

Manny paced the length of his room, grunting in an effort to suck air into his closed-up throat while fighting his fury towards an unknown Joe. Who was he? Where was he? He needed to get his hands on the dirty old man who'd dared to touch his Sifon.

The idiot must be older than him if he'd been married to Sifon's mom...or not. How old was Sifon, and how long ago had her story occurred? Was she still infatuated with Joe? The thought squeezed his throat, further making breathing difficult. He knew he'd been trying to dissuade her from wanting him, but imagining her in another man's arms, especially an older man, had him wanting to break things.

That bastard, Manny fumed, flexing his hand with the need to throw a punch, and equally, caress up Sifon's thighs. Breath left his mouth in a whoosh as he silently allowed the truth in — his fury wasn't necessarily directed at the unknown Joe, but himself.

Despite snapping at Sifon and pushing her away, her story had got him so furious because at some point, he'd not been imagining the faceless Joe touching her, but himself. He'd been furious at himself because he'd sat there and wished it'd been him in her arms.

It was painful to acknowledge, but Manny had always been honest with himself. His stormy fury stemmed from the fact that he felt even dirtier than Joe. Her stepfather had the excuse of grief and being blind drunk at the time; Manny had no excuse to have gotten so hard at her story he'd almost come at the table before flinging his seat backwards with a roar of self-disgust.

The front of his joggers soaked up the moisture that leaked from his dick while it strained with the painful bulge of his erection. It was a losing battle that he fought. He wanted Sifon. He needed to have her like his next breath, but then he suffered with what she wanted, which was something he couldn't give her. He couldn't give her fairy tale love; he was too old for that shit.

A sigh settled the decision in his mind. He believed after fucking her once, the whole novelty of it would evaporate, and he'd think clearly again without conflicting himself. Perhaps Sifon would realize that she preferred men her age after all. The thought left a bitter taste in his mouth as he marched to the guest room.

***

Sifon shrugged off Manny's fury once her breath returned to normal and cleared the table, refrigerating his untouched sandwiches and doing the dishes. In all that time, her body remained heightened in sexual awareness. It felt like her whole being hummed with the painful need to be tangled with Manny in the dirtiest, most intimate manner imaginable.

Sighing, she slammed the door of the guest room and plopped on the bed. Only now, Manny was probably too angry to look at her face. Being X-rated about her story had taken it too far; she couldn't explain how it had turned from confessing her dirty secret to recounting a fantasy.

Shame suffused her, eliciting a groan from her throat. This would surely shatter the tentative friendship they'd been trying to build, not to talk of the investment to Joshfon. As a shrewd businesswoman, Sifon had not been thinking at all about the consequences of her actions, she'd been too imbued in getting Manny to accept the obvious chemistry between them. It meant... Scoffing, she refused to think about Udeko and how onerous speaking to him would be.

She should have stopped pushing. She should have allowed Manny to come to her at his own pace. It would have been better having his investment and him in the long run than destroying all possibilities with her stupid story.

With a heart so heavy it threatened an avalanche of tears, she got to her feet, dumped her overnight bag on the bed and sorted out undies to wear before pulling off her nightshirt. She'd probably have to explain this event to Joshua. It was necessary that she did, but she wasn't looking forward to it.

Sifon stood without a stitch on, about to pull on her bra when the door burst open with so much force it bounced against the wall, a scream lodging in her throat together with her heart as she started and turned, instinctively covering her breasts with her arms and the bra. It was a useless effort.

Manny's gaze was like a direct heat source, burning everywhere it touched on her body. His eyes were dark with anger, and hunger, and pure lust. His chest rose and fell as though he'd just completed a marathon, expanding on every breath he took.

She stood there, not knowing how to react. All she wanted was to run into his strong, capable arms, but despite the pulse of want pounding through her veins, she hesitated. He was probably there to announce his displeasure and expound on how wrong they were for each other.

Swallowing with difficulty and shame dusting her heart, Sifon shifted her weight from one foot to the other, conscious that she stood naked, not just in the absence of clothing but in the fact that he knew her darkest secret.

"I, err..."

He marched towards her, eyes furious, but there was also something else. Before she could try to figure out the new element, Manny had her in his buff arms, his lips meting a punishing kiss on hers. She termed it punishing because his hold on her body was tight, and his kiss was an attack, like he was angry with himself for doing this, but his moan was helpless.

Struggling in his strong hold, she extricated her arms and hugged his neck, melting against the entire hard length of his torso, surrendering to him. His arms caressed her back, lowering to below her considerable buttocks to lift her, with her arms still around his neck, and lay her on the bed.

Manny stood back and allowed his gaze free rein over her body, his expression that of wonder, causing Sifon to bit her lower lip shyly with the double need to cover up, but equally, spread her legs for his roaming eyes.

She did the latter. And then she worried for his heart rate as it visibly accelerated until she could see the pulse in his throat.

"Fuck," he exclaimed, quickly pulling off his soft t-shirt to reveal his muscular upper half and a swirling tattoo, which was quite unexpected on an older man. She'd known he was buff, but seeing his skin and the salt and pepper hairs trailing from his wide chest to his solid belly and disappearing into his waistband got her tingling all over, eliciting a moan from her slightly open mouth.

At the tiny sound she made, his breathing became rougher and louder in the room, competing with the soft hum of the AC.

He shoved down his running pants, together with his boxer shorts, exposing the huge, hard length of his angry, dark dick. He stumbled forward as he kicked the clothes from his ankles, wedging his palms on the bed, with his face inches from her spread out pussy.

"Oh...oooooooh," she exclaimed as his tongue gave her a single, upward swipe that got her shaking and gasping, her head thrashing from side to side in the deepest pleasure.

"Did you just come?" Manny asked her with excitement and awe twinkling from his eyes.

Sifon covered her face but nodded. "Yes, daddy," she replied through her hands.

"Oh, shit," Manny groaned and with quick moves, he knelt on the bed in between her thick thighs, the head of his dick bridging the wet lips of her pussy. He rubbed the head on her clit, causing her to fling her head backwards in a groan while her hips jerked from the bed to meet him halfway.

"Damn it! I don't have condoms," he mourned while his hips kept moving, following the rub of his dick on her nub.

Sifon panicked. If he stopped because they had no protection, he would have time to rethink and perhaps change his mind.

"I've never done this without protection, and I'd just done my full physical months ago. I've not been with anyone since. Fuck, I want you so much," he panted, sliding only a few inches in and then pulling out. Sifon looked through bleary eyes as he used her pussy cream to pump the length of his hardness, the large purplish head popping up from his fist and causing him pleasure that left his mouth open.

"Me neither," Sifon gasped, hoping he took her response as meaning she'd not done it without protection before. "I want you to fuck me, daddy," she whined, and Manny lost it. Their passion was wild, a culmination of their dance around each other.

"Oh my...okay, sweetheart." He shoved into her, struggling through her tightness before making one huge thrust that had Sifon wincing and gasping in pain.

"What the..." His startled eyes clashed with her guilty ones.

She bit her lip, her eyes pleading, "Daddy..."

He rolled his eyes, as though calling him that messed with his control. "Baby girl..." He moved, hissing and biting his own lower lip as he looked between them to watch how he fucked her.

Sifon wished she could see, but just having him hover over her, finally feeling the fullness she'd craved and known only he could provide, was sending unimaginable pleasure hurtling through her body and made her come without warning.

She could feel the warm liquid leak into her arse crack while Manny kept pumping powerfully, this time more slippery, his balls smacking her arse. The room filled with the sound of wet, slapping skin, heightening the erotic aura that surrounded them.

"Fuck, baby girl, you're too tight," he gasped, his hips pulling backwards and pushing in deep, his arse squeezing in his effort.

"Don't you like my tight pussy, daddy?" Sifon asked, pouting at him while raising her hips to meet his delicious thrusts.

Manny shook his head, gasping and pumping faster, his muscular buttocks squeezing and releasing, his stomach muscles tightening as he pounded into her cunt, laid bare because his hands held her thighs spread.

"Daddy loves your wet pussy so much he's going to come wildly into it." She moaned and tightened her cunt walls in ecstasy as she fell over the edge, causing a groan from Manny as he stiffened for a moment and then slammed into her continuously, grunting and moaning his climax.

Sifon watched his expression, the helpless pleasure that had him frowning as he thrust, his slack mouth as he grunted, groaning as though in pain that he'd come. Her pride soared that she'd given him that. He let down her thighs, allowing them to sandwich his lean hips and then fell forward, still filling her. He balanced his weight on his forearms, his gaze accusing as he looked into hers.

"You lied."

CHAPTER TEN

Paradise.

It was the only way to describe the warm cocoon of fulfilment that engulfed them, and the desperate need that plagued them despite the many times they'd made love, barely having time to eat.

Amazing was the only way he could describe letting go of his inhibitions and accepting the explosive chemistry between them. He'd dreaded the aftermath of the first time, especially since he'd been blindsided with her virginity.

His accusations had her lashes falling over her expressive eyes, then she'd pouted, and he was a goner, even though she'd not known. Sifon said she was nearly 30; Manny thought it wasn't so far from 51. And the event with her stepfather, who was still alive and living in Uyo, had happened eight years ago. She'd told him that she hadn't lied about her stepfather; he just hadn't persevered to the end of the tale, where Joe had snapped out of his grief fog to push her out of his room.

Joe had moved out of the house the next day, asking her aunt to move in. The feeling of hatred for Joe had subsided to allow grudging admiration for the man's control. If he could see and touch his Sifon's luscious body, one he currently couldn't get enough of, yet was able to push her away, even in inebriation, then Joe deserved his utmost respect.

Manny was mad proud that he was the first man to breach her sweet cove. And it tripped his heart whenever she expressed her desperate need of him, pouting and calling him daddy.

Her name for him just blew his mind every single time. He couldn't explain the ground-shaking pleasure that coursed through his body, heightening his need for her. The effect of that word from her mouth left him wanting to consume her. He'd never thought he'd be one to be kinky, but, when she'd called him that, something had clicked between them; an acceptance and, perhaps, their own special dynamic.

There was no shame in it; rather, a wild, delicious heat of inexplicable need drove them to hours and hours of fiery passion. Manny had never experienced such blinding pleasure, even in his younger days when he'd be on a job and not have a woman for months. Then, it had felt like an obligation, even when he'd been married. More recently, his time with Irene had been more for the companionship than the sex; he'd enjoyed giving her pleasure and getting his own release, mostly to clear brain clutter.

But with Sifon...dear God. He turned to stare at her lovely, fresh face as she slept from their recent bout of lovemaking. It was all they'd been doing since Saturday morning. They'd only gotten up to snack, which had ended with him bending her over the kitchen counter and sliding into her very wet cunt, eagerly taking his hard length while his hands had squeezed and played with her fleshy buttocks.

They'd also taken baths. Manny had never had the urge to bath with a woman, but with Sifon...she'd pouted and asked if her daddy would bath her. He groaned at the memory and grabbed his hardening dick to control his desire, wanting her to rest.

"Shit," Manny muttered, his hand moving on its own accord, slowly rubbing his erection. He had been instantly aroused at her request and, of course, in the course of rubbing the soap on her soft, slippery body, he'd gotten stuck on her bounteous breasts, enjoying the tiny gasps from her mouth whenever he grazed her nipples.

He'd not wanted to do anything, not after losing count of the times he'd fucked her. But when he'd stood behind her to wash between her legs and she'd moaned, pushing her big arse against his painfully hard penis, while fucking herself on his fingers to completion, he'd snapped and thrust into her while she was yet to come down from her climax.

Another groan escaped his throat, his eyes startling open to find Sifon licking the mushroom head of his phallus, tight and shiny smooth since he'd grabbed the base to keep from coming from the memory.

"No, no, no, baby girl, you need to rest," he half-heartedly protested.

She shook her head and crawled to her knees, her beautiful, dark arse painting the air as a large heart shape when she bent over and swallowed the head of his shaft. A groan wrenched from his throat, slacking his hold at the base as his hips started jerking, sliding his pole into her warm, wet mouth.

"You know what will happen if you keep at this, baby girl."

Her eyes met his with her mouth full of him and she nodded. He spurted pre-come at the erotic sight and she moaned, licking it off with a pop and then using his hardness to tap her extended tongue.

"You're begging for it, baby girl," he gasped. "You want daddy to stuff you full of his fat dick, right?"

Her loud moan was response enough but she nodded eagerly, sucking his hard length with her mouth hollowed to give more suction. Manny hissed his pleasure and leaned to the right. Reaching for her thigh, he caressed up until his fingers encountered the thick cream gliding down from her cunt. His baby girl really enjoyed sucking him.

This was another part that blew his mind. She was so expressive, and her reactions to his touch just added to the already explosive passion between them. Manny reached her soaked cunt and moaned with her when he felt how entirely wet she was from just sucking him. He retracted his fingers coated with her cream and sucked them clean before going for more.

"You taste so sweet, baby girl. Daddy wants to eat your pussy all the time."

"Mmhmm," she moaned and nodded, moving her hips and tightening her cunt walls to try and suck his fingers deeper.

"Hmmm," he moaned as he sucked his fingers clean of her juice. "But daddy can't stand it just now. Come sit on my dick, baby girl," he commanded and she immediately complied, even though she lingered a bit as she swiped his cock one last time.

Flinging her legs over his hips, she squatted on the bed, aligning her cunt with his cock and slowly sliding down, her extreme wetness making the transition a smooth, delicious glide.

Moaning, they remained that way for a few seconds, her channel so tight he had to bite his tongue to keep from coming immediately. Then Sifon placed her palms on his chest for support and started moving. By this time, their desire had heightened to an elevated level that only climaxing would bring down, and so, with skin slapping skin, wet suction sounds, and Manny pulling her down to suck her nipples, they both crashed together. Silence filled the room, except their heavy breathing, and then Sifon started giggling.

"What's funny?" Manny asked with humour in his tone, his hand smoothing her short hair, spiked during their passion.

She leaned up on her elbow and looked into his eyes. The emotion in hers caused his heart to leap and lodge in his throat. He swallowed hard, his basic instinct prodding him to look away, to hide from the seriousness that might follow, but he held on, and saw as her eyes clouded over.

Sifon must have sensed his apprehension, but instead of confronting him, as he'd expected — all the women he'd known reacted that way when he dodged issues — her gaze lowered to his lips, and she licked hers before melding them to his in a soft, sweet kiss that had him tightening his arms around her curvy body.

Their eyes fluttered closed as they enjoyed the moment, then she leaned up again, eyes sparkling as though they'd never been clouded. "I laughed because you said we wouldn't do this again," she murmured with a smile.

"I did, didn't I?" he mock-pondered before tickling her without warning.

Giggles erupted from her throat while she struggled from his nimble fingers, consequently falling to the side, his dick slipping out of her warmth and wrenching a grunt from him. Her giggles ascended to a full belly laugh while she tried to curl into herself to avoid his fingers.

She looked like an angel in that moment, and his heart lurched at how beautiful she was. Sifon was a light he was realizing he needed. Another kind of fear engulfed his heart as she sobered up and cleared her throat. She did that a lot. It was cute, and the unconscious mannerism came with an attitude that belonged on someone his age.

"It's past five p.m.," she announced, her lashes lowering to cover her lovely brown eyes.

And he knew what the time meant. An end to their lovely time together. Manny swallowed hard, his heart thumping with the pressing need to tie her up. He didn't want her to go, but saying that might just give her the wrong idea.

"Yeah," he sighed and shifted close, cuddling her. "We've been in bed for more than 24 hours," he said, nuzzling her neck and inhaling her intoxicating scent.

Her arms crawled round his neck, softly settling her body on his. "Yes. I have to go home and prepare for work, and my aunt has clogged my phone with text messages and calls..." She paused, as though waiting for something.

His heart hammered, his breath hitching as he knew, but refused to acknowledge, what she was waiting for.

With a weary sigh, she completed the sentence. "And you should've been at the hotel since yesterday and hours ago today. I can't hold you back."

***

Sifon couldn't believe it was ending. Manny had refused to say anything. She'd untangled from his arms, bathed and dressed in the bathroom and stepped into the empty guest room to put on her makeup.

Her throat clogged with unshed tears. If he wanted her, he would have pulled her to his room after the many hours they'd spent fucking and eating. One of those trips from the kitchen could've ended in his room, but he'd always led them back to the guest room.

If he wanted her, he would have asked her to stay, or expressed some reluctance at her departure. But none of that happened. Reality had crashed in. It had been naive of her to assume giving in to their raging chemistry would make him keep her.

As what — a girlfriend? A mistress?

Sifon sighed, shaking her head as she soberly packed her belongings. She straightened the bed sheet and had to swallow a sob when she saw the crimson stain. With another huge sigh, she pulled the sheet from the bed, dumping the white load on the floor in the corner of the room.

Anything would have been better than only the hours they'd had, but she couldn't force him.

She met him pacing the length of his sitting room, and her heart leaped with a smidgen of hope; he seemed in turmoil.

Yet, when he turned, he said something totally unexpected. "Take my car."

"Excuse me? No!" she exclaimed when she understood what he meant. "I can't inconvenience you like that. You could just drop me somewhere. It's still day time, and I'll find my way home."

His pacing landed him in front of her, his breath brushing her face as she looked up. "I wasn't asking, baby girl. You're taking the Camry, and you'll use it until your car is fixed."

Sifon sucked in a breath, looking away to blow it out. His calling her baby girl had jerked a warm reaction from the pit of her stomach. When she turned, her eyes were curious. "Why?"

Manny fidgeted, seeming like a kid in that moment. "Because..."

"Are you ashamed to be seen with me during the day?" She asked it casually, but the possibility increased the size of the log in her throat.

With widened eyes, Manny sputtered, "Why the fuck would you think that?"

Sifon gave him an eyebrow lift, which got him losing his momentum.

"Okay," he sighed. "See, I've got to be in the office like yesterday, and I want you to be comfortable. There's no need changing your routine or suffering inconveniences just because my mechanic is the slowest there is in Uyo."

She chuckled and shrugged. "Is that the key?" She nodded to his right hand.

Manny narrowed his eyes at her, as though confused at her easy acceptance. "Yes." He handed it over.

"Is it parked outside?"

"Right by the gate. I pulled it out for you."

She nodded — he really needed her out of here ASAP. So, as business-like as possible, she stepped forward and hugged him perfunctorily, murmuring in his neck, "Thanks for a memorable weekend, Manny." His arms were just about to round her when she stepped back, smiled, and headed for the front door. Sifon wasn't one to dwell on bad experiences, but this one would hurt for a while.

CHAPTER ELEVEN

Manny missed Sifon the moment her arms left his neck from that last hug. The need to hold her had slammed into him as he watched her march to his front door. Then he'd rushed to the window to watch her get into the navy blue car and drive out of his gate, widening the caving hole in his heart.

He'd spent the night at his resort with the excuse that it'd been a while since he'd done that. But, in the middle of the night, because he'd craved her warmth and the comfort of her soft, pillowy body, he'd driven back home and headed straight for the guest room.

It still had her scent, and the memories of the hours they'd spent tangled in bed were so fresh, he could have been hallucinating. He'd cringed when he'd grabbed the bed sheet in the corner, but something had settled in him when he found the crimson smudge. It was a feeling of such profound possession it scared him.

The sheet held a concentration of her scent, and he'd been instantly aroused when he'd smashed the material to his nose, sucking in all he could and regretting that he'd not taken her to his room. So, the stained sheet remained with him, arranged by his pillow to preserve her scent.

He'd forgotten to get her contact, having misplaced her card. Manny sighed and leaned back in his office chair at the resort. Two days without her, her giggles, and calling him daddy was driving him mad. He still hadn't figured out what title to give her, because the idea of her being a onetime indulgence had vanished the moment his tongue had tasted her young, virgin pussy.

Why the hell had she left? She should have pouted, looked at him through her lashes like he'd gotten used to, called him daddy and clung to him, and he'd have crumbled like the walls of Jericho in a bid to keep her at his house. Why the hell had he not called her back when she'd marched to the door?

With a deep sigh, he sat up and grabbed his phone. He couldn't take it anymore; he needed his baby girl fix. But, what would he tell Joshua to get her number from him? Would she tell her partner about their wild weekend?

Manny was torn between wanting her to be proud of him as her lover and scared shitless of what people, especially his close unit who knew he was antipathetic to this kind of thing, would say. Fuck them, he thought. He was an adult, and he had a right to do what the fuck he liked. He owed no one explanations.

Joshua picked on the first ring, causing a lurch in his throat. He still had no excuse for asking for her number, and this was the first time after a while that Joshua had answered his call.

"Hey, pops," Joshua greeted, making him cringe. Manny was immediately reminded of his age, more pronounced now that he was panting after a younger woman.

"Hey, Josh, err..."

"I've been meaning to call you, but it's been busy at the office, and I've been running around for the marriage introduction, I kept forgetting. Thanks for loaning Sifon your car. She told me hers broke down at the Commissioner's party and that you were there to help."

Sketchy, Manny thought, his heart yearning for more; he wanted to hear the explanation she'd given that had made Joshua believe her story. Additionally, this was probably why he'd finally picked his call. He cleared his throat, sighing in relief because he now had an excuse to get her contact.

"Yes, I misplaced the card you gave me, so, I need her contact to give to the mechanic for when he's done, so that he can return the car to her house."

"That mechanic of yours that takes forever to repair a car," Joshua grumbled, eliciting a chuckle from him. "I'll text you her number and address, even though I believe that her car should be trashed, or better yet, dismantled and sold for parts. But she's attached to that thing."

Manny sat up, his interest piqued, his need to know more about Sifon having become an obsession in the past two days. "Umm...why is that?" he asked with all the casualness he could muster in his tone.

"It was her mother's," Joshua supplied distractedly.

"Oh."

"Let me text you her details. I'll see you one of these days."

Manny groaned in utter frustration when Joshua ended the call; he needed more. An SMS tone dinged in his phone and he grinned.

***

It'd been three days, and she had yet to get over the breathtaking weekend.

Sifon had berated herself for forgetting to get Manny's contact. But then, there was no way she could have recalled something as benign as exchanging phone numbers when every minute during that weekend counted. She had been busy storing up moments that would keep her warm in the cold days. She'd known, and even though she'd ignored it several times, she'd glimpsed Manny's reluctance to have anything more than that weekend.

That was why it confused her when he'd given her his car to use while hers was repaired. Had it been plain kindness, or was guilt involved? Maybe both, Sifon concluded. Despite his glaring reluctance, did he miss her a little? Because she'd been missing him, and the dreams had become more detailed, leaving her panting awake and wanting him to the point of tears.

"Sifon!"

"Hmm!" She jerked from her reverie, looking up to meet Joshua's concerned gaze.

"Are you sure you're okay?"

He'd been asking her that since the beginning of the week, and each time, another level of guilt settled on her shoulders. She was a bad liar, and avoidance could only take her so far, but she worried for Manny. If he had a problem with being with a younger person, he definitely wouldn't want anybody to know about their weekend.

She had no idea how Joshua had even believed the sketchy story she'd given him on Monday when he'd seen her with Manny's car.

Sifon nodded with a small smile, "I'm okay, just got lost thinking." They were in Joshua's office, and Sifon sat in one of his visitor's chairs while they handled orders. It was a typical Wednesday at Joshfon.

"Is it the car?"

His question caught her off guard, and her eyes widened while her mind remained blank of replies that wouldn't involve vomiting how awesome she found Manny.

"Err..."

"Hullo!" Dora sing-sang, walking in through the open door, dressed in jeans, a t-shirt and ballerinas.

Saved! Sifon thought, beaming a bright smile at her friend. Dora screamed and rushed into her open arms, hugging her close. Sifon held tight, too. She'd missed her friend. She knew it was the marriage preparations, but still, this was a time she needed their little heart-to-hearts most.

"My God, it feels like I haven't seen you in a year."

"I missed you, too," Sifon grinned, letting her go so she could hug her fiancé who'd been waiting, impatiently, to hold her.

Sifon watched as he pulled her close, kissing her so deeply she had to look away to breathe. When he was done, he pulled her to his seat behind the desk, making her sit on his thighs, her arm round his neck.

"I thought you weren't around when I didn't see your car outside."

"Err..."

"Babe, I told you Manny gave her one of his cars to use while hers was repaired."

"Say again?!" Dora swivelled her head to Sifon with her eyes bulging out of their sockets. "Is this true? How did this happen?" Her gaze on Joshua was accusatory. "You didn't tell me."

"Oh, must have forgotten," he muttered with a smile.

"Sifon, you've been holding out on me!" Her eyes gleamed knowingly.

If she'd managed to avoid the truth with Joshua, it wasn't going to happen with Dora.

Joshua scoffed. "Holding out how, babe? Everything isn't gossip material; her car broke down at the Commissioner's party, thank God Manny was there, he called his mechanic, offered her use of his car, and that's it." He nuzzled her neck, nibbling on her earlobe.

All the while Joshua simplified her weekend, Dora never took her eyes off Sifon's face, and her discomfort grew by the second.

"Sifon...you wouldn't hold out on your best friend, would you?" she pouted, making puppy dog eyes.

Joshua chuckled, assuming it was just Dora being Dora. "That reminds me, Manny called to get your contact yesterday," he pulled his mouth from his fiancée's neck to comment.

Sifon couldn't control her jerked reaction. She straightened in her seat, her eyes wide while her heart picked up beats. "He did?" she managed to ask in a croak, her throat having gone dry, hope expanding her chest. Then why hadn't he called?

"I bet she's wondering why Manny hasn't called?" Dora pointed out with a smug expression, which caused Joshua to look at her with a considering frown.

"Call? He said he needed the number for his mechanic, not for..."

"Are you going to tell him, or should I?" Dora grinned, wriggling her eyebrows while Sifon looked miserable.

What would Joshua think, she worried. "Err..."

"What am I not getting?" Joshua's eyes swivelled from his fiancée to her and back.

"My best friend is in love with your Uncle Manny," she announced quietly, her eyes still not leaving her face.

Sifon sighed, equal parts relieved that the cat was out of the bag and worried that Joshua might blow his top.

His eyes widened. "What?" he whispered, seeming disbelieving. "Is this...true? Or are you guys just pulling my leg again?"

She shook her head, shutting her eyes and opening them before nodding. "Yes, she's right. I'm in love with Manny."

"Holy shit!" Joshua leaned back in his seat so suddenly, he almost upended Dora from his lap, but he was quick to catch her. "How did this happen?" he asked in awe.

"Well..."

"Your birthday party, she saw him across the pool, and bam!"

"Oh shit," he muttered, his gaze steady on Sifon for a couple of seconds. Then his eyes widened, perhaps more than the first time. "Oh! Was that... Is he the...daddy?" He lowered his tone as he recalled last Friday when he caught her murmuring in her sleep.

"Daddy? Who's daddy?" Dora asked frowning.

"Oh, God," Sifon groaned, covering her face, embarrassment suffusing her with a wave of heat. This was worse than she could have confessed in the first place. So, with a breath so deep her bosom visibly rose, she decided it was time to clarify.

"I spent the weekend at Manny's place after the Commissioner's event. Um...we had sex..."

"Oooo," Dora exclaimed with a giggle, while Joshua groaned as though in pain.

"To be fair, I seduced him."

"And, Manny, does he...reciprocate your feelings?" Joshua asked hesitantly.

Sifon's gaze went from Joshua to Dora, who immediately deduced that all wasn't well, and before she could look sympathetic, she looked away.

"Well, um...Manny is struggling...with his emotions."

Joshua nodded. "Yep, he would. You're so young. Now I understand his attitude at that breakfast meeting. He was obviously fighting his attraction by being unnecessarily mean."

"So...you aren't angry, or...scandalized?" Sifon asked, giving him a narrowed eye look.

Dora chuckled, hugging him while he scoffed, "Nah, I know it's genuine because I've never seen you with any guy, you've never been flirty. And I like you for him, you won't let him get away with the shit he sometimes pulls. Besides, he's avoided women like the plague since Irene left months ago, and even when she wasn't being a bitch, he still wasn't happy."

"Err...what of his...wife?"

"That's his story to tell. But there's no need to worry about the ring; it's just for props," he winked at her with a wide grin, seeming pleased.

"Aww, I'm so happy for you, Sisi," Dora said, coming around to hug her.

"Don't celebrate yet. He is a most reluctant participant in this."

"It will turn out fine, I can feel it."

"And her feelings are spot on...most of the time," Joshua added under his breath.

"Joshua!" Dora exclaimed in fake anger.

She laughed with her friends, hoping deep down that Dora's instinct would be spot on this time.

***

"Sifon Akpan Alexander! You could be pregnant right now."

"Nothing I haven't thought about," she muttered, gulping down water from the bottle she'd just gotten from the fridge. She'd gotten home an hour ago, taken a bath, dressed in a loose house gown and been waylaid by her aunt, as she'd done every day since returning from Manny's house with a strange car. And after the session with Dora and Joshua, she'd mentally tagged Wednesday as confession day and in exasperation, she'd spilled what her aunty Felicia was obviously not expecting to hear.

"Do you have sense at all?" Then, her dramatic aunt clapped her hands together as though dusting off sand. "My dear late sister must have been mistaken to call you a precocious child. Or, maybe, you've lost that good sense since growing up."

Only since meeting Manny, Sifon thought as she trashed the empty bottle and returned to her room, her aunt trailing behind with litanies dedicated to her senselessness. She had indeed worried about getting pregnant, which was why she'd consulted her menstrual cycle app to confirm her cycle calculations to make sure she was on her safe period, and she'd booked an appointment with her gynaecologist for a birth control prescription and other check-ups. Telling her aunt all these would only make the woman see her as abnormal, which Sifon had gotten used to anyhow, so it was best to leave it that way.

Besides, if any mistake occurred, she was comfortable bringing up a child on her own. Of course, she would love to have Manny in the picture, perhaps as a husband, but she wouldn't kill herself if it didn't happen.

And that's exactly what she told her aunt.

Felicia looked scandalized at her niece, then angry. "You're...you're mad! What is wrong with you? Have you thought about what people will say?"

Sifon rolled her eyes at her aunt. A mistake might not have a chance to happen, not with Manny's restraint, plus, the visit to the doctor, she thought, falling wearily on her bed. "You've known me since I was born, have I ever cared about what people say or conventionality?"

Her question left the older woman speechless, because it was the truth. She'd never cared for trending things. When teenage girls were keen on adding extensions to their hair during Christmas, she'd returned home from school to request a low cut. She'd explained to both her flabbergasted mother and aunt that she'd rather help at her mother's shop than line up for a hairdo at the popular salon down the road. Besides, it was stressful to make a hairdo and difficult to discard. The thing was, Sifon only went for what she wanted. It was why she'd been a twenty-nine-year-old virgin, as none of the guys she'd met had been worth the hassle of sex or relationships. If she'd been conventional, she'd have been in several draining relationships already, all for the sake of appearances.

Felicia sighed and sat on the corner of the bed. "I recall when you got into the university newly, and that Toro boy was the hottest thing to hit the street, just graduated and handsome with all the young girls vying for his attention. It was gossip fodder for weeks how you told him he was too childish to handle you."

Sifon chuckled with her aunt as they recalled the incident. Her mother had still been alive, then. "That guy had, absolutely, no content to his name, yet girls were stabbing each other to be with him. I didn't get it at all."

Her aunt sighed again, her lips twitching. "Is it why he gave you a car...the fact that you might be pregnant?"

She curbed her laugh because her aunt looked genuinely worried. "No, aunty, he was just helping.

Besides, he's really struggling with liking me. I told you, he's a respectable man, and everyone knows he doesn't mix with young ladies. Even Joshua confirmed that this afternoon."

"And you don't think Joshua is just covering for his Uncle? See, men tend to stick together against women."

"Conspiracy theorist!" Sifon joked, laughing out loud.

"You do realize I want the best for you, right?" Her eyes searched Sifon's face. For someone who had never had a kid of her own, she was the most loving woman, the best substitute for her late mother.

Sifon got up from the bed and hugged her now standing aunt. "I know, aunty Felicia, and I appreciate all of it."

"Okay, let go before you rumple my dress," she chuckled and withdrew from Sifon's arms.

"Are you going out?"

"Mid-week service."

"Of course," Sifon grinned, following her to the sitting room.

"Which you've refused to attend," Felicia accused as she reached for the bolt of the door, the same moment as a tentative knock sounded on it.

"Are you expecting anyone?" It could only be for her aunty as she never had visitors; Dora and Joshua called before visiting.

"No."

"Could be Mr. James down the street," Sifon teased.

Felicia scoffed, "He knows I have mid-week service today."

"Aunty, aunty," Sifon teased again, playfully pinching her chubby arm. Then the door opened, and her smile vanished. There stood Manny.

CHAPTER TWELVE

Manny spent about two minutes with Sifon's aunt, but it felt like hours. In that time, he felt judged and persecuted from just her stare and scoffs. He'd magnanimously offered her the use of his car and rarely-used driver, which she'd surprisingly agreed to, and then she was, hesitantly, off to church. He got the feeling she'd have loved to stay back and dissect him, but she was too ingrained in church and routine.

"I take it you told her," he started off, while he tried to calm his speeding heart with slow breaths. Surprisingly, it wasn't from the fear of meeting her aunt but the sight of Sifon after three days, which had felt like years. He was excited to see her and confirm that she was as beautiful, even more so, than his imagination recalled.

She was dressed in a loose cotton gown ending above her knees, her hair in spiky disarray, as though she'd had her hands in it. Her breasts boldly engraved the soft cotton, making him swallow with difficulty at the sight of her hard nipples. The dress also draped over her round hips, and the picture literally took his breath away.

She nodded from the spot, too far from him. She'd taken steps back when her aunt had opened the door to find him standing there. And she'd remained tongue-tied since then, so he'd had to introduce himself while he gave her minute glances, trying to gauge what she might have been feeling, and honestly, he'd just been unable to keep his eyes off her.

His inability to find her house on Tuesday had been the reason he'd called his driver from hibernation and, as expected, the young man found the obscure place easily. Manny was vaguely glad he'd not allowed her to fend for herself the night her car broke down. The path to her house was quite bushy and lonely and a woman alone on public transport could inspire violence.

He'd never felt this awkward because of a woman. Manny was thinking he should have called before showing up, but his throat had clogged in trepidation each time he'd tried her number. With the way she'd left his house on Sunday, he feared she'd sensed his uncertainty and, perhaps, had given up on him, which was why he'd decided to pop up like this.

Shocking her had been part of his plan, but he'd hoped it would be pleasant enough to trigger a hug and a murmured 'daddy', a sign that she'd missed him as much as he'd missed her.

"You have a lovely home," he grated out, barely seeing any of the furniture pieces while she stood there, barefoot on the tiled floor, shifting her weight as though uncertain about his presence.

She cleared her throat. "What are you doing here?" Her gaze finally landed on his.

Again, his breath left him, causing his heart rate to pick up faster than it did when he used his treadmill. "I, err..." He scratched his beard and seemed lost for words. Really, what was he doing here? Why had he determinedly searched for her home when, deep down, he still was hesitant about them?

Sifon sighed, her gaze exasperated as she stared at him. He was sure she could see the frown on his forehead as his mind searched for an innocuous reason for his presence in her home. Telling her he'd missed her these past three days would be tantamount to naming what was happening between them, and he wasn't ready for that. Telling her he'd just come to see her and perhaps get a hug in between would literally mean a lot more than he was ready to give.

"Umm... We really need to discuss business, you know, about your company and the investments."

"What about it?" she interrupted, a certain hardness tainting her voice. He thought he saw a shadow of hurt in her eyes, but she looked away. When her gaze returned on him, it was clear of any emotion, and still, his heart hammered on.

"Err..."

"Please, sit down." She waved at the settee behind him and he did as he was told, feeling like a mumbling child. "Care for a drink? I hear guys like you are into vintage wine, the kind that appreciates with age."

"Guys like me?" he sputtered, feeling both insulted and flattered from her statement but unable to pinpoint where each fell.

"That's the only thing you heard from what I said?" She walked towards him and, without warning, sat astride his lap, instantly causing his semi-erection to blossom, as though it was aware that paradise was close.

"Hmm," she moaned, moving her big buttocks on his hardness in a suggestive manner.

His hands flew to her hips, where his fingers grazed the beginning of her huge arse. Manny hardened his jaws and held her in place. "That's not why I came here, Sifon."

She sat back, her eyes meeting his in mock shock. "It's not? I could have sworn it was. I could see the outline of your hardening cock in your khakis, and your eyes couldn't stay away from my breasts." She leaned close, inundating him with her scent, her hard nipples grazing his chest as her mouth landed on his neck, nipping and licking, same as he wanted to do to her. "Are you lying to me, daddy?"

"Oh, Jesus!" he groaned. His reaction was instant; it felt like his dick was aiming to bust the zip of his pants. Manny had no idea when his hands on her hips turned from holding her in place to moving her desperately on his erection.

Her soft mouth progressed from his neck to his chin where she rubbed against his beard like a cat before licking the corner of his mouth. He groaned and turned his lips to hers, catching her in a deep kiss that both settled and fired him up. His hands caressed down from her hips and grabbed her luscious bottom. In squeezing the globes, her dress shifted and he touched her skin. She was naked under the dress, and Manny went berserk.

He heaved, his muscles bunching as he laid her back flat on the settee. In his haste to expose her breasts for his seeking mouth, he tore her soft dress, and it added to the eroticism of the moment, especially with Sifon moaning her encouragement. While his mouth settled around her nipples, one after the other, his right hand made quick work of his belt buckle and zip, then his hard cock came out for air, or more specifically, for Sifon's dripping pussy.

Shifting closer, he invariably widened her legs, her foot wedged on the muscle of his upper arms as he plunged into her accepting hole. Her liquid heat surrounded him, sucking him in, her swollen channel strangling his hard pole. She was still so tight, despite her wetness, and it made him want to fuck it wide.

"Please, daddy, move," she whimpered, her whining tone sending maddening tingles through his veins. He had to bite his tongue to stay still despite her tiny hip movements.

"My baby girl wants daddy to fuck her?" he grunted, grinding his hips but not withdrawing his length. It was a move designed to drive her mad, but it backfired when she tightened her cunt around his cock.

"Yes, daddy, please," she moaned, using the wedge of her foot on his arms to raise her hips, trying to get him to move.

Panting, Manny leaned in, nibbling her earlobe and whispering in her ear, his eyes shut as he tried to control the urge to slam into her; doing that would end this delicious experience faster than he wanted. "This is going to be hard, baby girl. I'm going to bang you like you owe me money and you're paying me with your pussy."

Her reply was a loud moan and a warm flood of her wetness bathing his cock.

It broke the dam. Manny reared back and began plunging. "Oh, baby girl, you like what I said? You like dirty talk?"

"Yes...oh, yes!"

An avalanche of pleasure surged through him, sending his body shivering as though he suffered from a terrible fever. Manny knew he was close to the edge, but he still wanted her to reach another climax. It added to his pleasure, and if they went over the edge together, even better.

"I'm so close, baby girl," he muttered through his teeth as his control began slipping, and his hand slid from her breast, down her stomach to her mound, his fingers seeking her pleasure nub. He rubbed slowly on her clit, flicking it while he pumped into her.

Their moans mixed, a crescendo of their passion, and their pants echoed in the sitting room, blending with the wet, rapid slaps of skin against skin. Manny grunted when he felt Sifon stiffening, a sign that she was about to...

"Oooh!" she exclaimed, unable to control her tone as she climaxed, invariably dragging him along over the edge of mindless pleasure with his own groans, embarrassingly loud in his ears.

For a minute, he settled his weight on her body, holding her close and inhaling her scent. Her arms went around his body, as though she couldn't bear to let him go.

They were quiet for a while, and Manny was shocked to discover he was almost falling asleep when he jolted by her whisper. "This feels like you came here because you missed me terribly."

It was a joke. Her tone was light and tainted with humour, but his basic reaction, one he wished he could've controlled, was stiffening. His whole body went taut on hers, and in her usual perspicacity, she noticed, loosening her arms from his torso.

There was no point in remaining on her warm comfortable body, so he cleared his throat and got to his feet, pulling up his trousers. He watched as she scooted to a sitting position, pulling down her rumpled dress and trying her best to pull the upper part over her spilling boobs, not in shame but in modesty. A smidgen of guilt coated his heart as he recalled that his desperation to get to her breasts had caused that.

"I actually wanted to speak with you about Udeko. You can't do business with him."

Sifon scoffed and got to her feet, not bothering to hold together the rift in her dress. "I would appreciate any information on the man, but you have no right to tell me what to do."

Guilt for the whole situation and anger that she wasn't listening to him swelled his chest. "See here,

Sifon, there's no need to be sentimental despite what just happened—"

"Your driver is here, Manny," she interrupted calmly and walked to the door, quietly unlocking and opening it.

Light from his car flashed through the flushed windows of the sitting room, announcing the arrival of his driver. She must have heard its approach, or she probably had real good timing.

It was obvious, though, that he'd messed up, because she refused to look at his face as he passed by her on his way out of the house. Surprisingly though, she didn't bang the door the moment he was outside. She looked him in the eye and asked how much longer she had to wait for her car.

"I'm sorry it has taken this long. The mechanic had to order for the parts needing repairs from Lagos."

"Oh, okay. I'd like to have the bill when he's done." Her words didn't sound angry or offended; she was either emotionless or really good at controlling it, and Manny wanted to know which concerned her.

He sighed. "I'm taking care of that, Sifon. I want to."

"And I appreciate you, daddy," she smiled, causing his heart to jump double time, which made him breathless and ready to slam her against the wall, shove up her dress and take her again. "But this thing we have..." She drew close, but didn't step out.

Manny stepped inside, just over the threshold, shading her from view. He didn't want anyone seeing his baby girl in her present disarray. This was for his eyes only.

Sifon stood on tiptoe and kissed him, withdrawing before he could deepen it. "What we have is with no strings attached, so, I'd prefer to handle my bills." She gave him no chance to reply as she stepped into the house. "Bye, Manny." She shut the door quietly, and the only thing he could do was leave.

***

"I really wish I could come with you guys," Sifon whined while Joshua arranged his table, preparing to leave for the day.

"Well, you could if you weren't seeing this Udeko guy tomorrow, and I appreciate that you're doing this for the team. I'm uncomfortable about him, but then, uncomfortable has no place in business. Plus, your rule of leaving no stones unturned is ace."

Except, you'll have to be responsible for turning Manny, Sifon thought. She didn't want to bother Joshua with that titbit just yet, not when he was leaving for Dora's village right away. On Saturday, the next day, he would perform the early marriage rites, literally interpreted from the vernacular as the Knocking of the Door; wherein the groom's family introduces themselves and his intentions to the bride's family and the list of traditional prerequisites for marrying their daughter is given.

"Sometimes, I regret making that one of our core company values," she scoffed. "Some of these stones are decorated stumbling blocks."

Joshua stopped shoving his personal effects into his knapsack and laughed, leaning weakly on his swivelling office chair. "Jesus, Sifon, you have a bad mouth."

"Well, imagine this Udeko guy fixing a business meeting on a Saturday! What's his aim, who does that?" Sifon asked, her lips twitching because Joshua was still laughing.

"Let's assume he's such a busy businessman he can only entertain such meetings on weekends." Joshua gave her a comforting pat on the shoulder.

Sifon sighed, "Anyway, I'm just doing this to fulfil all righteousness, I already have a plan cooking in my mind. I believe it'll be for the best, especially with us needing three more Mack trucks like yesterday."

Joshua slumped back in his seat despite looking ready to leave. "I've been trying not to think about it, especially with our main truck currently spoilt on the road. But despite Doctor Umana being patient and understanding, even one new truck would make a difference; we'd just send it over, get Umana's consignment and allow the mechanic to take his time in repairing the spoilt one. Except, even if Manny decides to invest, the agreements and paperwork would take forever."

Sifon eyed his worried mien, refusing to even think about Manny investing. It now just seemed like a clash of interest.

"Please, don't keep my friend waiting. Stop worrying, I'll work something out."

Joshua shoved to his feet. "I trust you. And don't worry about not attending tomorrow, you won't miss the main deal." He came around the table, and Sifon got up to hug him.

"Take care, and kiss Dora for me."

"You don't have to ask." He grinned and left the office.

Sifon laughed. "On the cheek, though," she shouted after him, chuckling and shaking her head.

But then, Joshua popped back into the office. "You didn't hear this from me, but Manny isn't going with us today because of a meeting. He'll be arriving tomorrow morning. Okay, bye!" He disappeared again, leaving her laughing and considering the information with a fast-beating heart.

Hmm, she thought, she could pay him a surprise visit as he'd done to her. A groan escaped her throat as she flashed back on their passionate tangle. Sifon smiled, recalling the clothes she'd gotten from the drycleaners, which could be a change of clothes for her meeting with Udeko on Saturday.

Her smile widened because she still didn't have his number, and he obviously had no need to call her; it was better she didn't call him. She planned on working late at the office, perfecting the plan she'd intimated to Joshua about and then visiting Manny at an odd hour.

"Prepare to be surprised, daddy," she muttered with a mischievous smile.

***

"You've changed, Manny."

"Change is inevitable, the only fucking constant thing in the universe. Why is it such a shock that I've changed?" His exasperation was plain.

Irene attempted a pout, a glaring distortion of her over-made-up face, which reminded him of the perfect pout he craved from Sifon. And as expected, his mind had found a way to rope in Sifon, a constant in his life he didn't know how to handle.

The head cook, Mr. Marcus, had just brought to his notice that his manager was skimming from him. Apparently, one of the kitchen servers was a graduate of Accounting, a real-life numbers wizard, which his thieving manager, Charles, didn't know.

Charles had come in as manager when the former one, Ekwere, suddenly resigned with no explanation. His skimming had been clever, which was why he hadn't noticed, but Charles had always chosen the accounting wizard server to help him — Udoro, who Marcus explained seemed socially inept, a probable cause for his being chosen to photocopy the account spreadsheets.

Udoro had been keeping photocopies of the spreadsheets for himself, just for studying, Marcus clarified, but it had led to the server discovering huge discrepancies in the account, ones he finally shared with a fellow server who thought Mr. Marcus would give him a listening ear without losing his job.

Charles had taken a four-day leave to attend some vague family emergency. Manny warned Mr. Marcus and the two other servers not to say a word about it. He wanted to catch the thief unawares on his return.

So, he'd had a long, bad day, and the only visitor he'd have wished for was Sifon. Her calming presence would make everything better, and she might even have good ideas on how to handle the issue. Besides, he'd decided she was more than a no-strings hook-up. Embarrassingly, he'd come to this realization when she'd declared their relationship exactly what he'd wished it to be.

All he could think of was that it left her open to other guys, perhaps even younger men, and he'd have lost the peace and joy and amazing sex that came with her. He didn't care what people thought anymore. He wanted to be with her. When she'd refused his help with the bills for her car, he'd been slammed with the realization that he wanted to do things for her.

Manny realized that he wanted to spoil her rotten. He wanted to surprise her and hear her mellifluous laughter, the one that had become a balm to his soul. He wanted her soft body against his at night, and he wanted to wake with her in the morning, his nose buried in her neck and his cock in her pussy.

What he didn't want was this tasteless surprise visit from Irene. He sighed, promising himself that as soon as he took care of this nuisance, he was going to call Sifon and apologize on the phone...he also wanted her voice in his ear.

"How did you even get in here?" He refused to mask his exasperation.

"I have a key."

"I changed the locks, Irene," he snapped.

Irene huffed, rolling her eyes and getting to her feet, straightening her dress, a sparkling thing too short for someone her age. She had obviously come with the intention of seducing him. Manny scoffed, shaking his head. He now wondered what he'd found in her in the first place.

"I have my ways, Manny," she replied coyly.

"I don't know what that means, and I don't have the energy to deal with it right now, so, please, leave," he said at the same moment as the doorbell rang.

Manny frowned. "What the fuck? Is there a universal invite to my house that I don't know about?" The bell dinged again. He turned to Irene, whose frown announced her legendary anger, a consequence of not getting her way. "Pick your bag, woman, you're leaving." The bell echoed through the house again.

"God damn it," he huffed, marching to the door, wondering who it could be at this late hour. He wrenched the door from the frame, ready to harangue whoever he found on the other side, so he was left speechless when Sifon leaned by his door with a sexy smile for him.

"Hello, daddy," she whispered, drawing close and hugging him as though she'd not seen him in months.

It should have been a jubilant moment that Sifon was at his front door after a bad day, but he couldn't react from the instant dread that suffused his mind that she was there with Irene in his sitting room; this could destroy everything.

"Umm..." She interrupted his thoughts with a slow, hot kiss that left no doubt what was on her mind.

"Manny!" As expected, Irene showed herself, causing his baby girl to stiffen in his arms and move to step away from him, her eyes wide with hurt clearly reflected in them.

To avoid babbling an explanation which would make him look guilty, Manny grabbed Sifon around the waist and refused to let go. He looked into her eyes and, perhaps, the truth shone through, because she quietly picked up her overnight bag and walked in. Majestically, if he did say so.

"Oh, hey, Irene. Nice seeing you again," she greeted in a pleasant tone.

Irene rolled her eyes and scoffed. "Little girl, save your greetings for someone that cares."

Sifon smiled, "Little girl?" Her eyes widened, looking Irene from head to toe and back. "In that dress, who should be little girl?"

Manny coughed to cover his laugh at Irene's shocked mien. Sifon had on a corporate gown that ended below her knees and shaped her curvy body without being too tight. She looked like the businesswoman that she was, while Irene appeared to have impersonated a tramp.

"Good night," Sifon called out, strolling into the corridor leading to his room.

"Manny! How could you allow her to insult me like that? What about all the times we spent together, didn't they mean anything to you?" Irene had bulldozed through anger and had entered the manipulative stage, the one he'd always given into because he'd just wanted to avoid the drama.

"You shouldn't have been here in the first place. You broke into my house, and you think you have a right to insult my guest? You're lucky she's mature and a hundred times more woman than you. Get out of my house before I call the police." Manny had been avoiding anger, but her attempt to manipulate him against Sifon had been the last straw.

Huffing, she grabbed her purse, her anger returning in the form of threats. "You'll pay for this!"

Manny rolled his eyes and opened his front door. "Madam, get out." He banged the door when she huffed by. "Rubbish." He was changing his locks the next day.

He stood there taking deep breaths, wondering how Sifon would react or what she was thinking. With another sigh, he decided to face the situation head on.

* * *

Sifon had always hated the feeling of anxiety; the uncertainty of it, the waiting, and the fact that she couldn't control the outcome of the situation making her anxious.

After her mother's illness and subsequent death, she'd made sure every facet of her life was under some sort of control. She'd studied all the sides and undersides of her business before going into it, making sure she knew what to expect and a solution for it before it occurred. It had led to her not having the patience for paltry hook-ups with guys her age, because it seemed like those ones didn't know where they were headed or what they wanted out of life, and she'd had no inclination to suffer through their stumbles.

Joshua had proven himself different by being attentive to the ideas she'd brought to the boardroom table at the company they'd worked at together. Most of their colleagues had treated her with exasperation, calling her 'Vintage' behind her back as they thought she behaved like an old woman. And so, when she realized she'd need a partner for her business to have any chance of success, she'd flat-out chosen Joshua.

In her need to avoid any form of anxiety, her mild straightforward attitude had upgraded to frank speech no matter who was involved; it had led to her learning everything about anything. But with Manny... Sifon sighed and continued pacing the length of the guest room. With Manny, most of the safeguards she'd created for her protection had melted.

It amazed her that even when she saw his reluctance, felt it, was sure of it, she'd still been unable to stay away from him. She'd tricked her mind into believing she was just having fun when she realized Manny didn't want any strings to what they shared. The pregnancy scare had only lasted the length of her bath time. She'd missed her appointment with her gynaecologist today, being so busy at the office, but she planned to do a walk-in after her meeting with Udeko. The conclusion remained the same, though; she was able to raise a child on her own, and after scanning her brain for all it entailed to raise a child, her nervousness had dissipated.

But the fact that she was pacing Manny's guest room, wringing her hands and biting her lower lip, was a sign that she didn't have all the bases covered with him. If he wanted to get back with his ex, she'd not stop him, but she'd suffer a breakdown of monstrous proportions because for the first time in her life, she'd opened up herself to uncertainty, to vulnerability, to love and its uncontrollable nature. It was why she'd decided to walk into the door instead of following her first, raw instinct of running away. Manny was her kryptonite, and she'd always give him a chance.

Sifon's pacing landed her in front of the full-length mirror. She sighed and stared at her teal pencil-cut dress; the hue complimented her dark skin and the cut settled on her curves as opposed to being tight and uncomfortable. Women her age might regard it as too conservative, perhaps not sexy enough to get a man, but this was comfortable for her. After all, she'd dressed for work, not for getting a man.

She smiled at her reflection, realizing that her mind had kicked in with thoughts of her attire to calm her down and, indeed, her anxiety had reduced. If Manny hadn't wanted her there, he'd never have allowed her into the house.

A heavy sigh thundered through her body and suddenly, she could feel the tiredness of a whole day's work. She retreated to sit on the bed the same moment Manny cracked open the door, ratcheting up her heartbeat again.

"I've been looking for you." His voice sounded hoarse, and instantly, her nervousness drained in favour of concern for him.

She saw his eyes go to her bag on the bed before he walked to it, picked it up, and grabbed her wrist, dragging her from the guest room, further down the corridor to his room — larger, all white, and saturated in his scent.

Oh, dear God, she thought, her pulse pounding. These were new frontiers, which meant new expectations. Was he... Sifon took a deep breath and refused to worry, or even expect any change. Perhaps, just as he'd been kind with his car, so he was with his room.

With a calming breath, she focused on him and the fact that he looked absolutely stressed and drained.

"You should take a warm bath," she commented after watching Manny stand over her innocent bag for about a minute, just staring at it.

"Umm...okay." He stripped and did just that.

Sifon frowned. There was obviously something wrong, something more than Irene at his house. While he occupied the en suite bathroom, she went to the kitchen and prepared a tall glass of iced tea with a dash of whisky in it, designed to calm nerves.

Manny had on a loose pair of shorts and was sitting on the bed when she returned with the drink. She handed it over with a smile, pulled out her nightwear and retreated to the bathroom.

She climbed into the huge bed the moment she was done, shoved her legs under the duvet and smiled at a staring Manny.

"This is nice," he croaked, raising the empty glass.

"Hmm," she admitted, and patted her thighs, indicating he come lie down.

Manny understood. He dropped the glass, crawling up the bed to lay on top of the duvet, his head nestled on Sifon's lap. He purred with his eyes drooping shut when her fingers sank into his salt and pepper beard and combed.

"Do you want to talk about it?"

His response was scooting closer, eyes still closed, his nose brushing the silk of her nightie against her soft stomach, a deep inhalation and moan that vibrated his wide, muscular chest, which invariably sent thrills up her thighs and tingles to her pussy. She ignored her lady parts and blew out air through her mouth.

"Manny?"

"Hmmmm." His eyes opened, and he looked relaxed. "I'm sorry you had to see that. Don't know how she broke into my house," he grumbled.

Sifon bit her lip to curb a smile. He sounded like a petulant child. "Is that why you're stressed?"

A sigh blew through his body. "Well, my manager has been skimming off my money for months."

"What? That's terrible."

With rapt attention, her hands never ceasing their caresses, she listened to his predicament and his plan, which she agreed was best. There was no need for temper tantrums that might notify the guy that he'd been found out; it was better to have him back and relaxed before he was surrounded.

"My poor baby," Sifon crooned, grabbing his head and bringing him close to her bosom before she bent and kissed his temple.

"I thought I was your daddy," he asked with a smile.

"Tonight, you're my baby." She caressed his chest hair, pinching his flat nipple and bringing it to life. "And I'm going to take care of you," she murmured before sliding down the bed and taking his lips in a soft, tender kiss.

The kiss was unhurried, and Sifon led it. She nipped his lips, licking slowly and plunging her tongue into his mouth to tangle with his, loving the smoky whisky taste of his mouth. She grabbed his face and deepened the kiss but withdrew when he wanted to take over. She did this until he realized she was in charge.

Slowly, she pulled down the lace straps of her silk nightie, revealing her breasts, and smiled when Manny waited patiently even as his eyes smouldered at the sight of her boobs.

"Would you like to suck my tits?" she asked in a husky tone.

He nodded vigorously, shifting close to do exactly that, but Sifon shook her head. "Not so fast, boy." Her forefinger paused his movement by landing on his lips, which he kissed and tried to suck into his mouth. He needed her, and his desperation sent power and pleasure streaking through her veins.

"I want to take your mind off your stress, so, we are going to play a fantasy game. A game where I will have all the control, agreed?" Her eyebrow went up in question, and Manny's response was to slide down and lie on his back with his head on the pillow, eyes closed. With that simple act, he'd relinquished all control to her, and it turned her on more than anything.

At that moment, she wanted to fall back and let him have his way with her, but she swallowed her base instincts and continued with the role-play she had in mind.

She leaned close, her mouth to his ear. "Imagine you're this young guy at the University, newly admitted, and your female professor, an older woman who happens to be a family friend, visits for the weekend and goes wild for you when she catches you in the bathroom and won't look away from your huge cock."

Manny whimpered, his eyes shut tight, clearly into the imagery she was creating because his loose shorts were currently tented and damp where the mushroom head of his cock crested.

Her tongue licked the lobe of his ear. "I am that professor, and I want use of your body. Your parents must not know about this," she whispered, her fingers trailing a path from his broad chest and down his hard stomach but stopping at the edge of his waistband before returning, prompting a whimper from Manny.

"You need to agree with all I say, or else...I won't touch you where you most want me to."

He nodded, eyes closed. "Yes, yes, Prof, I won't tell anybody." He licked his lips as though anticipating what she'd do next.

"Good boy. Now pull down your shorts. I need to confirm that your dick is as big as what I saw in the bathroom that day." He quickly shoved them off, his cock hard and jerking. Sifon licked her own lips, curbing a moan at the sight of the smooth, hard length which had her pussy tingling and secreting cream.

Her voice remained moderate, almost a whisper, to create the atmosphere of them doing something taboo, something deliciously inappropriate, and though she was in charge, the situation she'd created was getting to her; she was extremely turned on.

"Hmm." She touched his dick as though inspecting it. Then she wrapped her fingers around it and rubbed, eliciting a hip jerk and a hiss from Manny. "Looks even bigger than that time I caught you touching yourself in my room when you thought I wasn't around." Sifon lined her body up with his, using her feet to rub the length of his hairy leg while pumping him up and down.

When the pleasure seemed too much, she left off. "You want me, don't you? You want me even though you shouldn't, but you can't stop thinking of sliding into my wet, dripping pussy and emptying your come in me."

"Oh fuck!" he exclaimed, enjoying her words and her lips kissing down his body to swallow his dick whole.

Sifon was lost, but not enough to forget she wanted to drive Manny mad with pleasure. Her lips fastened on the head of his dick and sucked hard with her hand softly rolling his sac, enjoying his groans and unconscious hip movements. She glided her tongue down the hard length, then she moved lower, taking his balls into her mouth and sucking while her hand worked up and down his painful-looking erection.

"Oh, God, it's too much...I'm going to..." Sifon ceased everything she'd been doing when she suspected he was so close, and giggled when he groaned as though in pain.

"Can I be your baby girl now? Because I need my daddy to fuck me," she announced in a whiny voice that got Manny shooting off his back and arranging her on her knees, body flat on the bed and arse in the air.

He slapped her buttocks and they jiggled, the slight pain turning into tingles that got her gushing more cream. As though he knew, Manny rubbed the huge globes and then slid down until he was buried in her soaked cunt.

"Sweet darling, you're so wet," he groaned, his fingers working in and out, making squelchy sounds. "I want to eat your sweet pussy, but I'm so close, I'd rather feel you around me."

At his panted words, she felt the smooth head of his cock line up at her entrance and then slide in, filling her up. Sifon's mouth dropped open in pleasure, a moan tearing from her throat as he withdrew and plunged back in so deep, she felt his balls slapping her pussy.

"Faster, daddy...harder," she moaned.

Manny grabbed her hips, raising them higher while he got to his feet on the bed, his knees bent at a half crouch, and then he fucked her, slamming in and out, enjoying the wet symphony of their skin blending with her whimpers.

She cried out, feeling herself pulse around his throbbing length. Her voice became husky as the build of pleasure grew to overload and everything shattered; her control, her emotions, everything she'd been holding back.

"Manny!"

His movements quickened, and he grunted his orgasm the same moment her knees wobbled and gave out beneath her. Manny followed her down, his weight a comfortable blanket of pleasure on her back while he kept moving above her, but slower.

"Oh, Sifon...fuck!"

Their pants blended, and she could feel the pounding of his heart on her back as he fell to the side before he drew her into a cuddle. And in that tender moment, all her emotions surged to the fore, and she had a verbal vomit.

"I love you, daddy," she murmured as she folded into his body, enjoying his warmth, but she immediately hated her sharp perception, because cold that had nothing to do with the AC prickled her skin as she felt him stiffen at her words.

Tears slid down her cheeks, and she was glad that she had her back to him because she was able to shove her face into the bed, stifling her sniffs. After several tension-filled, silent minutes, he still hadn't said anything, so Sifon faked a snore. She had no idea how long she lay like that, but it must have turned real because the next time she opened her eyes, it was morning.

CHAPTER THIRTEEN

I love you, daddy.

Her murmured words had blown his world to smithereens. Shame suffused his being for his inability to reply. He'd tried, even just to say something less overwhelming, but his throat had been as dry as he supposed the Sahara would be. Manny had endeavoured to curb his bodily reaction, but he had no idea if he'd succeeded.

Maybe she'd not meant it. Maybe it'd been in the heat of the moment because their lovemaking had been phenomenal, even more than when he'd discovered she was untouched. That was still a novelty to him, that he was lucky to be the first man to be with such a beautiful, fantastic woman.

There was an affinity between them he'd been ignoring that had exploded during the role-playing; it'd been more than the physical pleasure, it'd been spiritual, yet he worried.

Could he trust a woman enough to love her? Even when he'd been married, he wasn't sure he'd loved his wife. Manny had coveted her and had been proud to be the one to marry her. The fact that she, even in death, was the everlasting link of anger binding Udeko and himself, made him regret ever marrying her despite her alluring beauty. It'd not been worth the trouble in the long run.

What he felt with Sifon, what they shared, scared the shit out of him. He'd never experienced this sort of overwhelming emotion before, and he didn't trust it. Plus, Sifon was an amazing woman. She could have any great man, someone her age, so what the hell was she doing with him?

It made no sense that she genuinely wanted him. And then she'd gone and said she loved him? That was the height of it, and his hackles had risen beyond his ears, except he also suffered a stuttering hope that she meant it. But why would she say something like that? They were okay just going with the flow. He'd been about to wobble into the next step of perhaps calling her his girlfriend, but then the mention of love had made the very air he breathed suspicious, especially coming on the tail of finding out about his manager.

Manny sighed as he stared at her sleeping form at 5:30 a.m. His base instinct was to fold his bulk around her, shove his nose in her neck and stay in bed all day — all weekend — but he had a long drive to Dora's village for the marriage introduction. As Joshua's stand-in father, he could not miss the occasion.

With the plan to send her an SMS when he got to his car, he leaned down and kissed her soft cheek, inhaling her scent with the hope that it would tide him over until he saw her again.

He placed another kiss on her brow, reluctant to leave, but he forced himself to straighten and walk to the door. His heart twisted. Manny couldn't explain the dread at the imminent separation, when he actually needed the distance to analyse his emotions and the way forward.

Shaking his head, he closed the door with a soft click. He fought the instinct to return to her, or perhaps wake her and ask her to come with him. Straightening his white native wear, he convinced himself as he walked to his car that he really needed the out-of-town distance from Sifon to be sane again.

***

Manny's SMS couldn't have been any more unromantic if he'd tried.

I had to leave early for Dora's village. Please, drop the key in the potted plant. See you later. M

Sifon shuddered from the coldness of his tone, or perhaps it was from the AC's full blast on her damp skin. She shrugged as she moisturized and dressed up in ten minutes flat.

She refused to give her heart the permission to break just yet, not when she had a business meeting with a despicable man in an hour. There was time to sufficiently break down later, in her room, with many different bars of chocolate and a romantic comedy.

Letting out her emotions and confessing her love was like laying her vulnerability on a golden platter, presenting it as a most valuable feast, and having it rejected by the king. The only reason she was this composed at 9:31 a.m. was this meeting; she needed her wits about her even though she'd already decided on what to do. It was this policy of hers of leaving no stones unturned that had her here, and she presently hated it.

Sifon made a half part right of her hair's centre and combed her short, dark hair to frame her face. For confidence, she had on dangling jade earrings that complimented her green knee-length pencil skirt, under a peach-coloured peplum blouse with nude block-heeled sandals and a matching purse.

With the understanding that even the mind-blowing no-strings sex with Manny might be over, because who sounded that cold if they still wanted to see the person again, she made plans. It was a fact that it would take time to get over Manny, and Sifon was already eyeing frontiers that would keep her busy during her heartbreak.

The nights would be difficult, but nothing good lost is ever easy. Finding the perfect man after all these years and losing him prematurely because she couldn't control her emotions long enough to rope him in was solely her fault, and she deserved some form of pain outside her coping mechanism.

Udeko had fixed their meeting for 10:30 a.m. at his VIP club and lounge, but she pulled into his parking lot at the dot of 10. She remained in her car, taking deep breaths in a bid to shake off the melancholy that had settled on her when she'd dropped Manny's house key in the potted plant; the act had felt so final, tears had prickled her eyes.

A call from Dora dried the tears, her chirpy attitude splashing light into her gloomy heart. Another deep breath reminded her that it wasn't final, after all; she still had his car and she'd see him when she returned it.

Sifon, feeling better at the prospect of seeing Manny again, was just about to step out of the car when an ash-coloured Lexus SUV drove through the gate and stopped behind Manny's blue Camry. She had no idea what made her hesitate to open her door, but she was glad she'd followed her instincts. Not only did Udeko step out of the back, but Irene did, too, still dressed as she'd been at Manny's house last night.

The older woman looked livid as she marched after an exasperated Udeko. What was their relationship, she wondered, opening the door slightly to hear her ranting.

"...not taking this seriously. He threw me out of his house at that hour because of that whore. He has to pay!"

Sifon was glad that her car was sandwiched by two SUVs. Additionally, the glass was tinted, so she felt suitably insulated from notice. Besides, her heart had tripped at Irene's vindictive tone and the fact that it concerned Manny. What could she possibly do to harm him? Then she recalled the wrath of a woman scorned, and that she had Udeko on her side.

Udeko was a dark-complexioned, slight man, with a pot belly that didn't belong on his body. He was dressed in white shorts and a polo shirt, as though returning from a game of tennis.

And as if to confirm her thoughts, he snapped, "This isn't the right time for this, Irene. I have a meeting with her in a few minutes, I need to change from these."

Would anybody believe her when she said this? And by anybody, she meant Manny. Would he think she was seeking his attention? Putting herself in his shoes, she concluded that she'd not believe herself either, especially considering their predicament. So, she quickly grabbed her phone and clicked on the video app.

It wasn't clear, but the image was discernible, and with their shouting, the audio was fine.

"Well, you better do what I want before she suspects you when she sees me here," Irene gave Udeko a smug look.

He sighed while Sifon's heart thumped painfully, and the hand holding her phone shook and sweated.

"What do you want?"

"I want you to order Charles to clear his accounts."

"That's not possible! Don't you care about your cousin's wellbeing? As it is, the little he's been skimming is dangerous."

Irene huffed, not seeming to care about Charles. Sifon realized the conspiracy was to destroy Manny, and she'd unwittingly walked into it by liking him.

But she'd met Udeko before Manny, which meant then that the two men had history.

Why hadn't Manny told her this, instead of just ordering her not to do business with him? Well, not that she planned to, anyway. Being here was fortuitous as it gave her this evidence.

"Let's fast-track the drugs setup, then. Charles tells me that the industrial freezer at the back is perfect for stowing the bags, then we can tip off the police."

"Fine, fine! Tell Charles to meet me immediately. This meeting should be done in fifteen minutes, and..."

Sifon slid low in the driver's seat, saving the video and trying to comport herself after what she'd heard. She wondered if she should still go for the meeting with how terrified she was at the moment. Her hands shook so much, she had to drop her phone and wipe her palms on her skirt.

Driving out of there would seem suspicious, so she waited and watched as Irene marched to the SUV they'd arrived in and climbed into the back, flashing thighs that should be covered.

She remained in her car three minutes after the SUV had left and Udeko had hurried into his club. She tried Manny, Joshua, and Dora's numbers to no avail, perhaps switched off or silenced because of the introduction rites.

Were they lovers, and what else had they done to Manny while Irene had been with him? What could she do with this blurry video? On a whim, she sent it to Joe Akang, her stepfather, with a message explaining it.

Sighing in relief, she stepped out of the car, arranging her features to a serenity she wasn't feeling at all, and went inside the club. One of the workers led her to Udeko's office, a modern and comfortable space that she wasn't comfortable in.

* * *

The meeting was going nowhere, and Udeko wouldn't stop trying to feel her up. The sly man had moved her from his office to the VIP lounge, where he'd been able to settle beside her on the black settee. This was no business meeting; this was more of a fishing expedition, where Udeko kept fishing for information about Manny and his businesses.

At one point, she'd snapped. "Look, Mr. Udeko—"

"Call me Steve," he insisted with an oily smile, his fingers creeping up her thigh where her skirt had ridden up when she sat on the low settee.

"Steve, I don't really know much about Manny's business, but I know the man is wealthy. My friend is getting married to his stepson or whatever he is to him, I don't care. As for me, I'm looking for a retirement plan. This haulage business is not for women, I can't do for much longer, so Manny is my safety net. The man is old, single, and has no children, so he must be lonely, and I'll be the one to give him so much joy, he'll have no choice but to will his wealth to me."

Steve, aka Udeko, had laughed long and hard at her comment. Then, as though satisfied with it, he had begun asking her random questions about herself. Whenever she managed to shift the conversation to the business and possible investment opportunities, he would break in with questions so ridiculous Sifon was close to tearing out her hair from her skull.

"Do you like sex?"

She sighed in exasperation, "Who doesn't?" At this point, the pretence that this was a business meeting had evaporated, and Sifon only sought an opportunity to announce her exit.

"I hear Manny avoids sex. His medication makes his penis weak most of the time," he reported with a sneaky look.

Sifon wanted to slap him across his protruding mouth for saying such slander against her Manny. She took a deep breath, reminding herself that this man and whoever else he was in league with just wanted Manny's downfall, and it appeared it wasn't just in business. Once again, she wondered why.

"That's easy, there are young guys everywhere. I can always have a boy toy to service me when I'm horny. I do not depend on Manny for my satisfaction." The dirtier and more despicable she could make her replies, the happier Steve Udeko was.

Minutes later, Charles walked into the lounge, a tall, lanky fellow. She knew this because a server had announced his arrival before Udeko asked he be shown in.

Their conversation was vague, but she understood it because of the video she'd made earlier. As casually as she could, she turned on the recorder app on her phone, dropped it beside her purse and asked Udeko for the direction of the rest room.

The plan was to give them a bit of space to speak freely. And as though to better her plan, Udeko didn't point her to the restroom off the side of the lounge, instead directing a worker to take her down the hall.

Sifon took a minute to sigh and shake her torso to relieve some of the tension that had her neck aching. Disgust coated her tongue at all that she'd said just to keep Udeko satisfied, and the feel of his sweaty palm on her skin.

The tension had made her pressed, so she actually relieved her bladder. Her mind was in turmoil, and she planned to seek the truth from Manny about his relationship with Udeko and Irene, and why they would plot his destruction so heartily. But first, he needed to be saved.

When she returned to the lounge, Charles got to his feet, a sign that he was leaving.

Sifon faked surprise. "You're leaving so soon?" she asked as she picked up her purse and phone and smiled at Udeko. "I don't want it to seem like I'm the one chasing your guest."

"Ah, nothing of the sort. I had hoped you'd spend the day with me."

Her smile was wide as she shook her head, following Charles out of the lounge to the entrance and out into the sun. "Maybe some other time, I have another meeting in a few minutes. Perhaps we'll talk business next time?"

"Of course, my dear," he said, and then opened his arms, signalling a hug.

She felt as if hives were breaking out on her skin as he pulled her in, and she had to struggle to untangle herself from him, even her smile had dropped. She marched to her car and drove out while listening to Udeko and Charles' plan in depth, the drug plant and set-up that would occur at Manny's resort.

Her plan had been to have a quick shower at the office and change her clothes before meeting up with her stepfather, but after what she'd heard, she drove straight to his house while trying to call Manny, to no avail.

CHAPTER FOURTEEN

Manny wallowed in the feeling of contentment that blanketed him at the successful event of Dora and Joshua's introduction.

Dora's family were amiable and the list given to Joshua wasn't as exorbitant as the one he'd had to pay for his wife. Additionally, they were given a chance to argue the list, and the number of some items got reduced or slashed entirely. The only thing unarguable was the bride price.

It had ended with entertainment and an agreed-upon future date when Joshua, accompanied by himself and friends, would return to present the items on the list and the bride price.

Manny felt proud of Joshua like a father would, and in that time, he missed his dear, late friend. He'd taken time to tell Joshua that his father would have been extremely proud at how successful he'd become.

A vague thought slithered through his heart; for the first time in his life, he wished he had his own child. And when he imagined having a child, it was Sifon's image that flashed in his mind. This opened another thought path he'd been refusing to entertain; the fact that they'd been making love with no protection.

The only way he'd been able to keep that thought at bay, never bothering to ask Sifon, was to believe that she was smart enough to protect herself. Now, he wondered if she had indeed protected herself, and if she hadn't...his heart leapt.

His phone pulsed in his pocket, and he was reminded that he'd put his phone on vibrate mode, though there'd been no need for that as the village had no cellular signal. It was apparent that the signal was back, and he expected he'd have some messages and missed calls.

Slowing down, he pulled out his phone, clicked the tone back and placed it on the phone holder on the dashboard. Since it was dusk, Joshua was able to signal him with his headlight, and when he drew to the side on the main road, Joshua informed him he was buying fruits for Dora as they were cheaper in the hinterlands.

Manny smiled and nodded, using the respite to check his messages. Irene seemed to be the only person that had called and messaged. He sighed, wondering what the hell she suddenly wanted after being silent for so long. He'd thought she'd been out of his life for good, especially with Sifon in the picture.

He opened her messages, and his breath left him. There were pictures of Sifon with Udeko, with his hands on her in what looked like tender moments. His heart felt caved in; had she been working with him all along? Was this why Udeko had sounded so sure at Frank's party?

"Manny?"

When had he stepped down from his car? Joshua was beside him in a flash, but he barely noticed when the recording in Irene's message began playing.

"There are young guys everywhere, I can always have a boy toy to service me when I'm horny. I do not depend on Manny to be satisfied."

"What?"

"Sifon would never treat you like that! My friend is not a flirt."

Manny turned to Dora and caught Joshua nodding to her comment.

"Did both of you listen to the same recording I just played? Did you hear her tone? I suspected this all along, how could she ordinarily want someone like me?" he spat with so much disdain, his fear coming to the fore.

"But, Manny—"

"Oh, there's another one," he interrupted Joshua with a sarcastic laugh, playing the next recording.

"Steve, I don't really know much about Manny's business, but I know the man is wealthy. My friend is getting married to his stepson or whatever he is to him, I don't care. As for me, I'm looking for a retirement plan. This haulage business is not for women, I can't do it for much longer, so Manny is my safety net. The man is old, single, and has no children, so he must be lonely, and I'll be the one to give him so much joy, he'll have no choice but to will his wealth to me."

"I swear, Manny, Sifon is not like this. If she said this to Udeko, then it must have been for a reason. Think about it," Joshua pleaded desperately.

Manny's head shake was vigorous in stark disagreement. She'd insisted on the meeting with Udeko, even after Joshua had shared his dislike for the man and he'd tried his best to dissuade her. And hadn't he, just this morning, wondered what she was doing with him when she could be with a younger man? Now he knew.

Without waiting for any more reasoning from Joshua and his distraught fiancée, he jumped into his car and sped off while Joshua and Dora rushed to their car.

***

Sifon bit her lip, her nervousness making her unable to remain still as she sat in the car at Manny Resort's parking lot.

It was 7:56 p.m., and she was still in the clothes she'd worn for the meeting with Udeko; all she'd discarded were her sandals for a pair of flat slippers.

Time had been of the essence when she'd gotten to Joe's house. Without much questioning, her stepfather had worked in tandem with the urgency and fear he'd gleaned from her face and tone.

Now, everything was in place, and all she needed was Manny's presence. She knew Dora's village suffered from signal fluctuations, more absent than present, but by this time, she expected they'd have been done with the event and started heading home.

With a deep sigh to calm her nerves, she called Manny again, and whooped unconsciously when it rang. Her excitement dwindled when the ringing stopped and he hadn't answered, and then dread crawled up her throat when she'd called four more times without response.

Was he not close to his phone?

Another burst of excitement hit her when she decided to call Joshua, and he answered after the first ring.

"Joshua! I've been trying Manny, but he isn't picking up. Is he with you?" Sifon didn't even try to curb her frantic tone.

"Err...it's Dora, Sisi. Joshua's driving. Is everything okay?"

Sifon thought her best friend sounded edgy, but she had no time to dwell on it. "Manny isn't picking his calls, is he with you? I've called five times already."

"Umm..."

She could hear Joshua's deep-voiced whisper in the background, like he was telling her what to say.

"Umm...okay, hold up. Joshua says he's going to try to flag him down; he's right in front of us. I'll call you back." And she ended the call in a hurry.

It never occurred to her that Manny should be calling her back, not Dora, she was just happy to have spoken to one of them, anybody close to Manny. Despite her innate self-sufficiency, she acknowledged in that moment that she needed Manny's comforting presence.

The man commanded all the space in her heart, and she always felt protected with him. Now that she'd confessed how she felt for him, it appeared all the other emotions connected with Manny were crawling out of the dark spaces in her heart, ready to let in light after so long.

True to her word, Dora called her back, strangely asking that she call Manny and that he'd answer her call. Sifon frowned. Not only had the chatty Dora sounded subdued and ended the call quicker than the last time, her request was weird, too.

Sitting up straight in the car, she licked her lips. Refusing to entertain the dread growing in her chest, she dialled Manny's number, placed the phone on her ear and waited.

It rang for so long, she was sure it would end without an answer, so when he picked the call, it took her a few seconds to speak, and the only thing she said was a relieved, "Manny."

"What do you want?"

Sifon frowned, not entirely understanding his snappish tone. Then she recalled he might not have the number of her second line, which she was using to call him.

"It's me, daddy." She instilled her pout in her tone because she'd missed him and sorely needed him in that moment.

"God damn you! Don't ever call me that again. You've played me for a fool this long, but not anymore."

Her frown deepened and her heart rate increased, yet she comported her tone, her go-to reaction when things seemed out of control. "I don't understand, Manny, care to explain?"

"Cut it out, Sifon! There's no need to act anymore. How could you do this to me? How the hell are you this evil, to fool Joshua for the years you've worked with him?"

The dread had turned into tentacles choking her breathless. She had to clear her throat to croak out the words, "I still do not follow." And even with his words tearing her soul into pieces, she worried that he was worked up and driving as she could hear road sounds through the phone.

"I saw pictures of you being cuddly with Udeko today. And before you deny it," he interrupted the beginning of her explanation, "I heard recordings of your conversation with him."

"What recordings?" Her voice cleared a bit in her indignation; what had that weasel of a man done?

Manny scoffed, "Did you or did you not tell Udeko that I'm your retirement plan? That you had younger men to take care of your sexual needs? Oh, and that you were only ever interested in my vast wealth, did you or did you not say these words?"

Instant recall and realization drained blood from her head. It appeared she hadn't been the only one with the smart idea to record their conversations; Udeko had, too. Sifon was sure he'd edited the questions that led to her answers and had sent the dirtiest parts to Manny, who'd not trusted her in the first place.

The people that knew her would instantly deduce that she'd not meant those words and that she must have said them for a reason. Joshua, Dora, Aunty Felicia and Joe knew her. She'd hoped Manny would take the fifth spot; the man that she loved and had surrendered her control and exposed her vulnerability to, something she never did.

"Cat got your tongue, huh?" His smugness came through loud and clear. She could even imagine the smirk on his face for supposedly catching her in a lie.

Sifon refused to blame him. Even though he hadn't given her the benefit of doubt to demand an explanation, she would give him one. It was obvious he didn't know her at all; plus, two wrongs didn't make a right.

"Um...so, will you give me a chance to explain?" she asked in the calmest of tones, hoping that he'd simmer down, hoping that for what they'd shared, he'd give her a chance.

It could have been only seconds of silence, but it felt like hours of doom to Sifon as she waited for her fate. She understood that this was it; this could make or break them, with no chance for even a platonic friendship.

"No, I won't," he replied, his conviction a weight on her ear.

Her heart plummeted into her stomach in dejection, the crashing of hope a deadly thing as pain seared the length of her throat down to her stomach.

She inhaled to control the pouring tears and not let them colour her tone as she spoke. "Umm...okay. Err...I'll drop your keys...umm, car keys at the reception. Yes...err, the car is parked—" She cleared her throat and forged on, her fingers fighting a losing battle with the flow of tears gushing from her eyes. "The car is parked at the rear parking lot of the resort."

"What the—"

"Thank you for everything," she said in a hurry and ended the call, not wanting to hear any more hurtful words from him. She dropped her head on the steering wheel and cried like never before.

***

Manny wished... He deeply wished that he could travel back two hours in time to erase his distrust, or perhaps a whole month to erase his hesitance and all the stupid questions he'd ever had about Sifon's genuineness, because that was the root cause; the reason he'd swallowed the rubbish about her sent by Irene.

How could he not have seen how pure she was? He scoffed at himself. He'd seen her purity, had been given it on a platter, but he'd chosen to suspect it. He'd suspected a chance at happiness.

Even as he'd spoken those hurtful words to her, deep down he'd known he shouldn't have, but he'd allowed his past experience to spur his tongue. He'd allowed his deep mistrust for women to cloud his judgement, and he'd rejected reasons contrary to what he'd wanted to see.

After the call with Sifon, it'd taken him an hour of hard driving to get to his resort. Unconsciously, he'd wished to see her one last time before she left, and from the way she'd told him about his car, he'd suspected she was already at his resort, but why?

Nothing could have prepared him for the police he'd encountered, waiting at his resort to question him about dealing hard drugs. The two cops said they were not really asking but were waiting on their colleague to bring an order to search his property, and that if he was telling the truth, Manny had nothing to hide.

It looked and smelled like a set-up; even though he'd cut those ties long ago, he knew they would find exactly what they said a 'good citizen' had tipped them off he was hoarding. Manny suspected Udeko immediately, and he needed no one to tell him that the pictures and recordings of Sifon were part of his evil plan.

The third policeman returned with the warrant to search his resort; specifically, the industrial fridge at the back, used to store raw food like beef, fish, and vegetables. But just as he thought he was done for, another set of force men appeared, and they didn't seem like they'd just arrived.

They couldn't have just arrived when they had covert videos of Charles, his manager, looking around suspiciously while he shoved several bags of what he supposed were hard drugs into the deep corners of his huge fridge.

The police tried to wave off the video and indict Manny, saying he must be in league with his manager, but the other force men, who'd introduced themselves with authentic Naval IDs, provided another video of Udeko and Irene planning to set him up. The video was grainy, but the people in it could be identified, and Manny did so. Then there came a recording of Charles and Udeko speaking, finalizing plans to set him up that night as opposed to waiting till the next day.

Sweat poured down Manny's face despite the police instantly cooperating with the Naval officers, who already had Charles, Udeko and Irene cornered in their respective locations. All the cops had to do was arrest them. And with the Navy involved, Manny was sure there would not be any issues. Udeko's money would not get him off, not with the physical evidence against him. Then there was the fact that Charles and Irene were singing like nightingales in custody; they were claiming Udeko put them up to all they'd done.

It was a miracle that all this drama occurred without any suspicion from his resort guests. These things brought down businesses when guests got wind of any kind of fraudulent connection, but all was handled quietly. Statements were taken from only his staff that knew about Charles' dishonesty with his accounts, and their stories collaborated with Manny's report.

After returning from the police station where Udeko and his cohorts were held, he'd driven his car to the rear parking lot, hoping that Sifon had yet to park his car, but it was there, dashing his hopes as the rare blue paint of the Camry gleamed in the parking lot light.

Manny had no time to mourn the loss of his baby girl because his phone rang. It was Joshua, calling to tell him one of the naval guys wanted to see him. He frowned, wondering why a naval officer was still on the resort premises when everyone had supposedly left an hour ago; it was 11:30 p.m. already, and Manny wanted to go find Sifon and grovel.

Joshua rushed towards him from the front of the reception where a man his age stood. Manny noticed the officer was taller than him and sported a fit body that rivalled his for someone their age.

"Manny, this guy is the one that led the team. He says he wants to speak with you."

"Do you know why?" Joshua shook his head in reply.

With a deep breath, he approached the man and shook hands with him.

"With all the drama, we weren't introduced. My name is Joe Akang, Sifon's stepfather. She asked me to give you this." He dropped the car keys for the Camry into his numb hand. Before he could vocalize his question, Joe continued.

"She was too distraught to drop it at the reception."

"Shit," Joshua muttered behind him. Manny was speechless, his tongue feeling like it had swollen to twice its normal size.

"I was too glad to meet the man whom Sifon had given her heart to, the man stupid enough to throw it away." Joe's tone had gotten hard at this point, staring daggers at Manny, who held the keys as though confused.

"I really am stupid," he croaked and glimpsed Joe's shock at his words. Manny shook his head with a sad smile. "No need to be shocked. I am the most stupid creature on God's green earth. All I've done is give her grief after grief for loving me. She chose me. Damn it, she chose me," he whispered, his voice clogging with unshed tears as he realized he'd never chosen Sifon.

"Do you know where I can find her?" he asked Joe.

"Her number is switched off," Joshua provided. "And my fiancée will probably never forgive you," he muttered.

"Dora, right?" Joe asked Joshua, who nodded with a proud smile, exactly how he should have been proud about Sifon.

"She told you about us?" Joshua seemed awed.

"Yep, she told me everything," Joe eyed Manny as he replied. "You see, Sifon is like her mother, God rest her beautiful soul, especially in matters of the heart. It took years of pouring my heart to her, of dedication, because this was a once-in-a-lifetime kind of love I couldn't afford to lose, before she finally surrendered. It was unfortunate that she died, and I will live the rest of my life mourning her."

"Sifon has more tenacity than her mom. She didn't date for the heck of it, she viewed it as a waste of time. She was sure of what she wanted and never hesitated to go for it. And you were it, Manny."

"I want to apologize," he exploded, the pain and guilt like a ball of fire in his chest, determined to burn him from the inside out. "Damn it, if you could just tell me where she is, I'd grovel, for the rest of my fucking life, I'll grovel and appreciate and treat her like the queen she is," he cried, uncaring of the curious glances he was attracting.

Pity might have flashed in Joe's eyes, but he wasn't sure. The man was taller than him, and the tears in his eyes might have skewed his sight.

"Like I said, she's even more tenacious than her mother, and self-reliant and stuck on her decisions when she makes them. I'm not sure there's a chance for you, Manny."

CHAPTER FIFTEEN

"Give me something, Joshua. Help me out here," Manny pleaded in obvious desperation. It'd been over a month without his baby girl. He cursed himself every time he recalled her watery breaths the last time he'd spoken with her. He'd caused her pain, and he couldn't forgive himself for that.

They were in his office at the Resort, where he spent his days because he couldn't bear staying at his house, which was overrun with memories of her.

Joshua eyed him, his gaze taking all of him in. Manny knew he noticed a stark difference in him. His usually groomed looks were careless and rough now. Mr. Marcus, his new manager, had told him so. But Joshua said nothing.

"I already told you. She's in Lagos, processing her mother's shares which Joe had been holding onto for her all this while. Did you know Joe was a voluntary retiree?"

Manny took a deep breath to curb his temper. Even though Joshua had told him this piece of information about her, every time he asked, a new detail always slipped in, and he lived for those new details.

"I didn't know," he croaked, rubbing his hands over his face and down his now overgrown and mostly white beard.

"Well, he did it for Sifon's mother, who hadn't even asked. Joe says he wanted to spend every available moment with her," Joshua chatted on as though he wasn't aware of what Manny was waiting for. He did this all the time, his own way of punishing him for hurting his friend.

"That's nice," he inhaled, fighting to curb his impatience.

"Yeah, and he thanks God every day that he'd had that chance with her, unlike you who's lost yours." He turned a smirk on him, crossing his leg over his knee as though thoroughly enjoying his suffering.

Manny leaned back in his chair with a humourless chuckle. "I see what you're doing. Whose side are you on here, Joshua?"

"The side of justice."

"Right," Manny nodded. He totally deserved the punishments meted to him for how he'd treated Sifon. "Will she ever return?" he asked, his tone sober while staring unseeingly.

Joshua sighed. "I don't know, Manny. Some of the shares have been liquidated, and they are worth some cool millions. She's even ordered two trucks for the company; they should be arriving in a month."

"Oh." Pride filled his heart at her accomplishment, but pain smeared the good feeling; he should've just invested in the company when he had the chance. "I can still invest in Joshfon, you know."

Joshua scoffed. "You make it sound like you weren't going to. Of course, you will, but the offer will be renegotiated since she's already gotten what we'd desperately needed."

"Fair enough," Manny nodded. "So, give me her email. I just need to let her know how sorry I am," he pleaded. Sifon's phone numbers had remained switched off all this time.

"Take it up with Dora."

He had. He'd even taken it up with Felicia, Sifon's aunt, and the woman had given him a piece of her mind. That woman was mean. She hadn't spared him, and at the end, she'd told him exactly what Joe had said that night. Nobody was willing to break Sifon's trust like he'd done.

"I'm sure she won't miss your wedding, if you'd just fix a date..." He withheld himself from snapping 'already' — he still needed to be in Joshua's good books.

"Dora is considering a Christmas wedding."

Manny couldn't control his gasp. "That's more than a month away." His dismay was obvious.

Joshua shrugged as though he had no say in it. "She's my queen, her wish is my command," he said, giving him a pointed look, one he swore he might never stop seeing on Joshua's face. One he wouldn't mind getting if only he had his Sifon back.

***

"Joe?"

The man groaned into the phone. "I swear, between you and my new young tenant, I can hardly breathe," he muttered to himself, but Manny heard and vaguely wondered what that was about.

"Sorry," he said, not meaning it at all, despite Joe being the only one that seemed to have a bit of pity on him. "I wanted to personally inform you that Joshua and Dora's wedding is on Saturday, five days from Christmas."

"Yes, I know, Manny." His exasperation was obvious. "And I still don't know if she'll make it. Considering how busy the roads are at this time of the year, I wouldn't advise she travel."

His heart plummeted. "Okay. But you'll tell me if she does, right?" He didn't care if he sounded desperate; he was desperate.

"Of course, Manny. Talk later, bye."

***

Sifon pointedly ignored Joe's fixed gaze as he ended Manny's fishing call in a hurry.

"You need to see him. He's losing it, and I think you've punished him enough," he reasoned. "You don't want him to have a heart attack, do you?"

She licked her chocolate-covered fingers as though she had no care in the world while her heart hammered so loud, she wondered why Joe hadn't heard it. "Joe, please. If I recall, you were so angry at how he'd treated me, I feared you were going to kill him. What changed?"

"Ev—"

"He's probably putting himself in this Manny's shoes."

Joe swivelled so fast Sifon feared he would tumble. His gaze widened at the short, round, very fair-complexioned young lady walking out of his kitchen with a plate of chocolate-covered croissants. He looked like he was seeing a ghost.

"What the fuck? What are you doing in my kitchen?"

Sifon gasped as she witnessed her prim and proper stepfather use a cuss word. For all her years growing up with him, she'd never heard him curse.

"I come bearing delicious chocolate pastries, and I had to transfer them from the pack to a plate," she grinned and winked at him, and Sifon coughed to cover a laugh when Joe looked like he was about to pop an artery.

"I gave you no permission to enter my house," he ground out through clenched teeth.

"I did," Sifon spoke up. "I asked for these pastries from your other tenant, the one with two kids. What's her name...?"

"Agnes," Mandy, the imp who seemed to enjoy torturing her stepfather, provided. "And I'm her assistant. You see, with two kids and a demanding business, I double as her babysitter and delivery person when it's called for." She placed the plate of pastry on the table close to Sifon's reach.

Sifon moaned in pure bliss as she took a bite from one. "Hmm, so hot and creamy and chocolaty. They have become my ultimate craving. So, stop being angry, Joe."

Joe's sigh was exasperated. "I'm not angry. But you need to tell him about the baby," he said pointedly. "Give him a chance..."

"Told you," Mandy sassed. "If it were him, he'd want to be given a second chance," she said, folding her arms under her bountiful bosom and lifting a brow at Joe.

"Why, the fuck, are you still in my house?" Joe snapped.

"It's nicer than mine, that's for sure," she replied glibly, grinning when Sifon laughed and Joe stormed out of his sitting room in a huff.

"Oh, wow," she said, calming from her laugh. "Sit down for a bit, Mandy. I think I like you."

Mandy snorted and sat. "You should, I've been delivering your drug of choice for three days straight."

"Hey, don't blame me. I'd not have known this slice of heaven existed if your friend wasn't suffusing the whole apartment block with the aroma of her baking," she said finishing off the third of five croissants.

"That's true, though," Mandy laughed. "I'm afraid for my weight, especially since my chef cousin is arriving soon. Between the two of them, I could explode from decadent food. Thank God I'll be leaving for training soon."

Sifon chuckled, even though she noticed that Mandy didn't sound happy about leaving. "You like him, don't you?" She'd have been blind not to notice a reluctant male and a very interested female, the exact same situation she'd had with Manny.

"Is it that obvious?" Mandy asked with an adorable cringe on her face.

"Maybe to me, since I suffered the same situation a couple of months ago." Sifon smiled through the ache in her chest, the one that had become permanent since the night of his hurtful words.

"Manny," she supplied, nodding in understanding. Silence suffused the parlour, and then Mandy looked Sifon straight in the eye. "How old is he?"

"Joe, I take it?" Mandy nodded. "Forty-eight. He was a few years younger than my mother, and they were madly in love."

"Oh." Her tone sounded so subdued, it broke Sifon's heart, and she immediately regretted adding the last part. "Why, then, does he act like he's seventy?" Mandy sniped, seeming to recover almost immediately.

Sifon laughed. "I really like you. And when I said they were in love, I didn't mean you don't have a chance. In fact, I believe Joe is fighting his feelings for you. It's been almost eight years since she passed, and he hasn't looked at another woman in that time."

She shrugged. "Okay," she said, looking everywhere but at Sifon.

"Can I ask a personal question?"

Mandy's gaze finally returned to her. "Aren't you worried about what people will say? You know, a young woman like you being with an older man?"

Mandy shrugged again. "The heart wants what it wants. It's really nobody's business."

Sifon nodded, hiding a smile. Shockingly, she'd been worried. With a loss of conviction that, perhaps, Manny wasn't for her, several unimportant worries had jumped into the cauldron that left her sleepless most nights. Mandy didn't know it, but she'd just restored her confidence.

"What about you? Will you give Manny a chance?"

A deep breath thundered through her rapidly changing body. "I believe I will."

CHAPTER SIXTEEN

Dora and Joshua's wedding was held late in the afternoon, so the reception at Manny Resort dragged from the evening into the night.

Manny couldn't believe Sifon was actually there. She looked cool and absolutely stunning. He'd had to blink several times to confirm she was the one sitting in the third row in church. At one point, his heart had almost beaten out of his chest when their gazes had clashed; hers were aloof, and Manny died a thousand times for putting that look on her face.

Her dress was a rose-coloured flared number with a deep cut in front displaying her ample cleavage. His cock jerked at the sight, eager to harden as though it recognized its benefactor despite the distance and circumstance.

He'd lost track of the ceremony because he couldn't take his eyes off her. And when it was over, she slipped away through the crowd, managing to take a picture with Dora and Joshua and escape in Joe's car before he had a chance to speak with her.

If not for courtesy, Manny would have driven off after the car, abandoning the bride and groom at the church. But he controlled himself, following through with his responsibilities and arriving at the decorated resort garden with the wedding party.

From then on, he relinquished all control to the wedding planner and Mr. Marcus, who made sure everybody got what they wanted; what he wanted had yet to appear. Had she returned home with Joe? Would she avoid her best friends' reception because of him? Guilt pounded the walls of his stomach as he reasoned that what he'd done to her sure deserved avoidance, even at the risk of offending best friends.

After roaming the first few minutes searching for her, he'd had to stop and answer questions from the event planner. When he was done assisting some high-ranking guests to their seats, he noticed that more guests had arrived, so he began the rounds again.

Just when he was losing hope, he spotted her at one of the more shadowed tables set in a corner of the tent, sitting in between her aunt and Joe. Manny stumbled as the effect of her knocked the breath out of him. He really was a stupid man to have been reluctant to receive her love, fucking given to him on a gold platter.

Manny stayed back and felt satisfied just being able to watch her. He'd missed her terribly. Just sharing a large tent with her, knowing she was only a few feet away, gave him a joy he couldn't explain.

But then his heart squeezed in dread when he saw her look extremely uncomfortable when food was placed on their table in front of her aunt. She quickly slammed her hand over her nose and struggled out of her seat, using the nearest exit from the tent.

He was outside before he even realized he was moving. Her dress billowed behind her as she briskly walked towards the unsuitably unlit path of the garden, a section in which he was building a playground and kiddie pool.

His heart stuttered. That area was unsafe with building materials strewn all over. "Sifon. Baby girl!" he called, jogging after her when it seemed she'd quickened her steps.

But then she stopped and frantically searched for something in her purse. Manny reached her, his chest heavy with dread as concern for her clouded his mind.

"Baby, what's the matter?" His eyes followed her movement until she found what she was looking for, a wrapped roll of peppermints. She was so consumed with peeling the wrapper that her purse dropped while her hands shook uncontrollably.

"Let me." He collected the mints from her, worried when she whimpered as though in need. He peeled it easily enough, pulled out two tablets and tenderly fed them to her.

Their eyes met as her tongue extended for the minty tablets. Both of them hissed when her tongue touched his finger, then she was moaning in relief as she sagged on the iron railing around the unfinished swimming pool.

Manny wanted to drag her to him and never let go, but he had to be patient as it looked like she'd just avoided a crisis. He picked up her purse, replacing the things that had spilled, and stood next to her, staring at him.

Apparently, she had on her contacts; they made her eyes bigger and almost luminous.

"Marry me, Sifon," he blurted. It was absolutely not what he'd planned to say. He'd wanted to grovel first, apologizing until she forgave his stupidity; then, and only then, would he have proposed.

Sifon gasped, eyes widening as her chest rose and fell rapidly. "You have the nerve," she whispered, a bit of her anger slipping through.

"I'm sorry. So sorry," he stammered, moving closer to her.

She stepped back but couldn't go any further as the iron rails stopped her. Her frown looked worried. "For what?"

Manny took a deep breath. "For never choosing you when you were always choosing me. Even when you'd been at risk, you chose to expose a plot against me. Even when I was being a fool, you could have called off the raid you'd arranged, but you didn't... God, baby girl, I'm so sorry, for all I said." He couldn't bear not touching her anymore, so he did.

He grabbed her arm, pulled her close and engulfed her in a hug that was his first step to redemption. His worries dissipated when she didn't pull away, and hope bloomed when he felt her inhaling him. Then she started sobbing, which threw him right back to worrying.

"Oh, sweetheart, whatever it is, I'll take care of it for you," he swore as he pulled her from his body to inspect her face and her body, worrying that she must be ill to be acting this way.

Since it was getting cold in the garden, the dry air of harmattan blowing her beautiful hair and sticking it to her glossy lips, Manny pulled her to his side, walking carefully and leading her to his room at the resort.

***

Perhaps it was the pregnancy hormones that had made her lose control like that, but she couldn't deny that an overwhelming feeling of happiness had blanketed her at his sudden, unexpected marriage proposal, causing her bout of tears. And Manny's confusion and desperate need to solve whatever was her problem was so adorable, it melted her heart.

Sifon had heard of Manny's instant turnaround once he'd realized she'd not been the one fooling him, but his former mistress and Udeko. She'd heard how desperate he'd been to apologize to her. Even Aunty Felicia had called on his behalf when she'd been in Lagos liquidating some of her mother's shares; a shock, since she might have been more furious than

Joe, and had threatened to castrate Manny whenever and wherever she saw him.

Dora had been angry, too, and she'd reported with glee how he was suffering, looking unkempt and bothering Joshua every day for information about her. But Sifon had not celebrated, because she hurt for the pain he was going through, yet remained scared when she recalled how quickly he'd been willing to believe lies about her. It was what had kept her away.

He'd not trusted her love for him.

But his eyes had communicated so many things every time she'd caught him staring at her in church. It was like his gaze was stuck on her, because theirs clashed every time she'd turned. His eyes on her had felt like a brand, and she couldn't deny how awesome it'd made her feel that the man of her dreams was looking at her as though he'd die if he looked away.

The man of her dreams currently looked flustered in his impeccable suit after settling her on the edge of his bed.

"Can I get you water, anything?" His eyes pleaded, like he wanted her to need him.

She did need him, just not how he thought. She sniffled and patted the space beside her. "Come sit."

Manny narrowed his eyes in confusion but seemed eager to sit beside her, and then he was up again, as though she'd burned him. Hurt bloomed then subsided when she realized he wanted out of his suit jacket, tie, and cufflinks. Her man was dapper in whatever he wore.

Then instead of returning to the spot beside her, he went on his knees in front of her, helping take her shoes off, and she was reminded of the first night she'd spent at his house.

"I hesitated in trusting and receiving your love because I have a deep mistrust of women. My late wife cheated on me with Udeko and tried to spoil my business."

Sifon gasped, understanding dawning on her why he would easily believe the lies peddled about her. If his own wife could do that, he probably assumed one who'd been a no-strings-attached girl, who'd pursued him, could do worse.

"I'm sorry. I didn't know."

"It turns out Irene was working with him the whole time. And though I'd tried to stop you from meeting with Udeko, it all turned out for good, because I'd probably be in jail right now. So... Thank you, Sifon." He looked into her eyes, his gaze reflecting more than gratitude.

She dropped her eyes, suddenly feeling abashed at the attention he was giving her.

"I need to tell you everything, baby. I was a smuggler when I was younger, and Joshua's dad was kind of my mentor in the game. Etuk had some other young people under him and Udeko was part of us, but Etuk was partial to me and it made Udeko jealous, and he was always trying to sabotage me."

Sifon swallowed hard as her heart thumped, knowing this was a deep secret that Manny, perhaps, had never told anyone. It meant he trusted her, to tell her this.

"Etuk was aware of this, and he'd always tell me not to think I would be a smuggler forever. So, before I even met my wife, Bukky, he was already putting me on to business investments from the money we made. Then he told me about a woman he'd impregnated, and that he had a son whom he loved and didn't want joining smuggling like his bosses had done for their offspring."

Manny sighed. "Long story short, Etuk messed up, losing most of his money in a deal, and he knew he would be killed, since the person involved was a notorious criminal that everyone knew was vindictive. So, Etuk gave me what was left of his money and asked me to take care of his boy, to protect him from the smuggling life. He covered my tracks when I fled, even though Udeko and the others had been adamant I remain, as the notorious criminal wasn't out for me but Etuk."

"I ran. I ran with Bukky, whom I'd been married to over two years. It took me another year, during which time my businesses had begun sprouting profit, to realize Bukky was in league with Udeko and they were defrauding me, kind of like what Charles had done."

"I'd known he'd coveted Bukky, but I'd not known Bukky had coveted him right back or I would never have married her. But I was young, and I'd taken Udeko on any challenge he'd put out, one of them being who'd succeed with Bukky. I'd married her without even knowing her. When I caught her and threatened to have her arrested after our divorce, she ran and died in a car crash as she was heading to Udeko. He hasn't forgiven me since then."

Manny's head dropped on her lap. He seemed drained after sharing his past and the cause of his deep mistrust of women, Irene having proven him right. She forgave him for thinking the same of her. For a man to carry that kind of load around, it must have been difficult as he fought his feelings for her this whole time.

"I'm sorry for disappearing. Perhaps I should have been more patient."

Manny shook his head before she was done. "No, darling, no. You did nothing wrong, and you never have to hide or withhold your emotions from me. Be furious with me whenever you feel like I'm messing up, because I might be way older than you but, baby girl, you've taught me a fucking lot of things."

A giggle escaped her mouth. "You're still cussing."

"God, I missed that sound, your giggle, your scent." He leaned in, placing his temple on her breasts. "If you want me to stop cussing, I will, whatever you want me to do, I'll do it, just don't ever leave me again, please. I love you, Sifon. I love you terribly, and missing you, not being with you, was the worst thing that has ever happened to me. So, marry me, already, sweetheart, make me whole again."

That overwhelming feeling surged in her chest again, and tears prickled her eyes. "Don't you think it's too soon?" she ventured, trying to confirm that he was sure, because she'd known he was the one that first night by the pool.

"Hell no, baby. I've wasted enough time being hesitant instead of grabbing you before someone else noticed how awesome you are. I love you, Sifon."

She would never tire of hearing him say that. "I love you too, daddy."

Manny groaned at her words, tackling her with his shoulder and laying her flat on the bed. "God, I missed you," he growled, making quick work of discarding their clothes.

He growled again as he stretched his naked length over her, sighing as though he'd come home when her arms wrapped around his neck and her thighs widened to fit him.

Her pussy pulsed with the need to be filled by him after so long. She'd missed him terribly, and his hard cock just jerking at her wet entrance was driving her wild.

"I want you, daddy."

"Baby girl missed daddy's dick?"

Her nod was vehement. "Yes, please, now," she gasped, her need pounding in her veins as though she'd explode from waiting.

"Okay, baby, open your legs for me. Let daddy slide into your wet, sweet, pussy."

Sifon whimpered and did as she was told. She grabbed his hips and tried to shove him in quicker than his slow slide. "Daddy!" she moaned, pouting at his slow torture.

"You never answered if you'd marry me, or..."

"Yes, yes, I'll marry you!" she exclaimed with a frown and pout that got him laughing.

"That's better," he said and started pounding into her.

The build of pleasure was instant and her orgasm blew through her without warning. She whimpered while Manny murmured gibberish into her ears in his pleasure. It was, indeed, better.

"Fuck, I love you, baby girl, my sweet baby." He scattered kisses on her face and neck as he twisted his hips and shoved his hard length into her, hitting a particular spot that had her screaming her climax again.

"Oh, daddy, it's too much, it's too...oh!" she gasped as his cock sliding in rubbed on her oversensitive clit, totally erasing what she'd been about to say. She thrashed beneath him as he lowered and caught her lips in a searing kiss while his hips quickened, his moans and hers blending into each other.

Sifon felt Manny stiffen, then he wrenched his mouth off hers to expel his grunts as he poured his seed into her.

"I love you so much, darling. I'm sorry I didn't say it enough." He fell to the side and dragged her into his body, kissing her face and neck as though he wanted to gobble her up. "I regret not allowing myself to love you as you deserve. And as I missed you, I wished all those times we'd fucked, that I'd planted my child in you."

"I really felt it when I watched Joshua at the marriage introduction. I wished he was my kid. And when I imagined having kids, it was you that flashed in my mind. My subconscious already recognized you as mine. I was the one holding back, and I'm sorry."

All the while he spoke, his hands and mouth never stopped moving and touching her. A log wedged in her throat, and tears prickled as that overwhelming happiness increased.

"Are you saying you want babies?" she croaked, leaning back to look into his eyes.

"Baby, why are you crying? If you don't want kids, we won't have them, but we should probably think seriously of protection." His concern for her was cute.

And even with her tears, she giggled, "Answer me, Manny," her fingers combing his trimmed beard and loving the feel of the bristles against her hand.

He frowned. "You're confusing me, baby girl, like when you were desperate for peppermints. What was that about?" he asked, recalling the incident at the garden.

She widened her eyes in exasperation and he grinned, bending down to kiss her.

"Yes, I want children with you."

"Then we are having one in less than seven months," she announced in glee.

Manny laughed, "Why do we have to wait seven months before trying for a baby?"

Sifon sighed in exasperation then whimpered when he sucked her earlobe into his warm mouth. "You're not listening. The seven months is the time left before I go into labour."

It took a little while, but it finally sank in. Then he got to his knees on the bed, his eyes so wide she worried they'd fall out of their sockets. "What? I mean, umm..." His palm tentatively went to her stomach. Sifon could feel it tremble. "Oh God, oh God, I'm having a kid, sweet God, I'm having a baby with you."

His happiness was uncontained. He grabbed her in a hug and kissed her so thoroughly she felt molten. Manny pulled her back, his hand trembling over her stomach, his awed eyes fixed on her slightly swollen abdomen, one that wasn't quickly noticeable because she was chubby. Then, lying on his back, his hands never having left her body, he pulled her onto him, making her sit astride his body. His hands caressed her thighs and her arse and somehow ended at her stomach again.

"Fuck, why do you love an old man like me? What did I do right to be gifted with you?" He looked amazed.

"Perhaps we are blessed to have found each other. Most people live their whole lives without meeting their soulmates, and some avoid their soulmates due to social hang-ups." She thought of how they could have missed each other because of society's expectations; thank God Manny had let that restrictive consciousness go.

"But as for why I love you," she leaned over him, her mouth a whisper away from his, "I hear wine is sweeter when it's older." She kissed him, and it turned into another furious lovemaking session, one that had them both climaxing together, screaming their pleasure without care of being heard.

When they could catch their breath, Manny shoved off the bed as though he was being chased. He opened the bedside drawers, and Sifon assumed he was looking for something.

"Manny?"

"Yes, baby," he said as he ransacked his overnight bag, his arse a thing of exquisite beauty. Then he turned, grinning with a black box in his hand. "Found it."

"Hmm, you have a nice arse, but your front is even better." Her eyes rolled down his body to his semi-hard cock, then she licked her lips.

Manny groaned and jumped on the bed, eliciting a squeal from her. "Focus, baby," he growled, kissing her hard before rolling to the side to grab her left hand and slide the shiny diamond ring on her fourth finger.

"You're mine, for eternity."

Sifon giggled, loving the adoring look on his face. "Oh, I get to drink this tall, sexy bottle of fine wine for all time."

EPILOGUE

Five Years Later

"Why did I love the sight of you and Junior so much?" Sifon gasped while she hurried out of the flared sky blue dress she'd worn for Dora and Joshua's second child's dedication.

Manny swallowed hard, helping her pull the dress down her rounded hips, equally loving the sight of her huge baby bump, the one that got him so hard every time.

"Because we wore matching suits?" he supplied, dragging her into the space between his open, naked legs. His cock hung hard and straight, leaking moisture as though weeping in anticipation of sliding into her wet, sweet pussy that he'd never tire of.

"Could that be it? I was so horny when I saw you coming down the church stairs, holding his hand, with both of you in fitted cream suits and sky blue shirts, and your cabana hats...hmmm."

He kissed her bump, lifting her left foot to the bed while sliding his tongue to her navel, following the dark, thin line demarcating her smooth, hard stomach down to her fleshy pussy.

"Oh...fuck," she moaned, her hands tightening on his shoulders.

"You need to lie down," he murmured, loving her immediate reactions to his touch. He tenderly helped her lie down, spreading her pussy to his eager tongue. "So, you were telling me about being horny?" he prodded while he took small licks of the copious amount of cream glistening on her swollen cunt.

He loved that she was so horny during pregnancy; it was his favourite time. She'd given him a son, and now, they were lucky to be having a daughter, one he hoped would look like Sifon.

"Yes," she moaned, her hand pushing his head deeper in between her open legs.

Manny chuckled against her pussy, "Yes to what, baby girl?"

"Umm..." She licked her lips, wearing an adorable frown on her brow as she tried to recall what they might have been talking about. "Is Junior okay?"

This also happened, sharp changes of subject as she spoke whatever had entered her mind in that moment. Now she worried for their four-year-old son, who had his chocolate skin and was an adorable little man.

"Yep, he's with your aunt Felicia, who threatened bodily harm if I even ventured to take him. We have all night, baby girl, you can scream as loud as you want."

"I always scream as loud as I want," she teased, lifting her hips to meet his hot mouth.

"That's true." His words were muffled against her dripping cunt.

"God, it was a great idea to wear matching suits. I loved that everybody admired both of you. Well, except that tramp who tried to..."

Manny scrambled to hover over her, lifting her right thigh and sliding into her cove, pausing not just her thought process but his. He didn't want her getting herself worked up by women who didn't matter. His aim was to keep her satisfied and happy and relaxed.

"I love you, baby girl."

Her gasp of pleasure and orgasm was so spectacular it threw him over the edge. He shivered his release into her, loving that she still managed to hold him close despite the obstruction of her baby bump.

"I love only you," he whispered in her ear, as he turned and spooned behind her.

"I love only you, daddy," she murmured, her last word slurring in sleep.

Manny smiled. He couldn't wait to meet their daughter. He couldn't wait to wake in the morning to enjoy moments with the love of his life. He'd never thought fairy tales were real, nor imagined it could happen to him, but it had, he thought, as he held his wife and fell into blissful slumber.

Thank you for reading Fine Wine by Emem Bassey. Please leave a review on the site of purchase.

There are two more books in the Age Is No Bother series coming soon.

Subscribe to our <u>newsletter</u> to keep up-to-date with all Love Africa Press book releases.

ABOUT THE AUTHOR

Emem Bassey loves romance in all its glory, be it books, movies or music, especially when blended with action, adventure and magic, definitely with a plus size heroine. She staunchly believes that the world is already filled with too much tragedy, so she writes to entertain, to give relief and lighten the heart. She has written over twenty stories, most of them are published on Okadabooks. She is the author of the popular Duct series, Baby's Angel and Unromantic series. Two of her stories are published in two Love Africa Press Anthologies. She lives at Uyo, Akwa Ibom State and is a ghost to her neighbours.

OTHER BOOKS BY LOVE AFRICA PRESS

Love and Hiplife by Nana Prah
Be My Valentine Anthology: Volume 2
Bound To Liberty by Kiru Taye/Kai Tyler
Her Golden Eyes by Holly March

CONNECT WITH US

Facebook.com/LoveAfricaPress
Twitter.com/LoveAfricaPress
Instagram.com/LoveAfricaPress

SIGN UP TO OUR NEWSLETTER
https://www.loveafricapress.com/newsletter